ANNE OF SUMMER HO

ANNE OF SUMMER HO

Clare Rossiter

Chivers Press
Bath, England • G.K. Hall & Co.
Thorndike, Maine USA

This Large Print edition is published by Chivers Press, England, and by G.K. Hall & Co., USA.

Published in 1997 in the U.K. by arrangement with the author.

Published in 1997 in the U.S. by arrangement with Laurence Pollinger, Ltd.

U.K. Hardcover ISBN 0–7451–8851–6 (Chivers Large Print)
U.K. Softcover ISBN 0–7451–8889–3 (Camden Large Print)
U.S. Softcover ISBN 0–7838–2045–3 (Nightingale Collection Edition)

The text of this Large Print edition is unabridged.
Other aspects of the book may vary from the original edition.

Set in 16 pt. New Times Roman.

Printed in Great Britain on acid-free paper.

British Library Cataloguing in Publication Data available

Library of Congress Cataloging-in-Publication Data

Rossiter, Clare.
  Anne of Summer Ho / Clare Rossiter.
    p.   cm.
  ISBN 0–7838–2045–3 (lg. print : sc)
  1. Large type books.   I. Title.
[PS3568.08473A56   1997]
813′.54—dc21
                                                    96–48193

CHAPTER ONE

The midday sun was warm and high overhead, making the interior of the coach close and humid. I had long ago given up hope of finding a comfortable position on the hard leather seat. Every bone in my body ached and I had bitten my tongue several times when the vehicle lumbered over a stone in the road or trundled through a pot-hole, left by the winter rains.

Two days ago I had left both London and parents to accompany my new husband to his country home and begin a new life as a member of the aristocracy; no mean feat for a merchant's daughter, but my education had been as good as a boy's and my mother had seen that I lacked no ladylike accomplishment. The Summers had never accepted a title and were even more proud of that fact, than that they were related to almost every noble house in England, something that impressed my father mightily.

Because of the uneasy state of the country, my wedding had not been so grand an affair as my mother would have liked, but Harry Summer's friends from Court had been there to see him well and I had enough bride clothes to delight any maid's heart and a dowry that could not fail to please my husband.

At thought of Harry, I glanced out of the open window, still not used to the sight of this handsome devil-may-care that my father had chosen for my groom. Tall and well made, he was at ease in the saddle and I could admire in secrecy from the dark interior of the coach. The bright sun turned his long hair to gold under the broad-rimmed hat and the tip of a white ostrich feather brushed his cheek. As though sensing my gaze, he turned to look at me and lift his hand in careless salute.

'He's a proper Cavalier and no mistake,' approved a voice from the other seat and I looked across at my maid.

'I had thought you asleep,' I said.

'Not in this instrument of torture,' she remarked feelingly, rubbing and stretching her cramped limbs. 'If we get to this Summer Ho, we'll have to think ourselves lucky.'

As though the fates were listening, the coach lurched violently forward, swayed and then crashed down onto its side, accompanied by the screams of the horses and shouts from the outriders.

For a moment I lay dazed in a heap on top of Meg, before the door, which had changed places with the roof, was opened and Harry peered in anxiously.

'All right, Anne?' he asked. 'Then, I'll pull you out if you'll stretch your arms to me.'

With his booted legs planted firmly either side of the opening, he reached down and,

2

grasping my wrists, lifted me easily out, then did the same service for Meg.

Bruised and shaken, but not really hurt, we stood in the roadside and made much of our injuries, while the men released the terrified animals and examined the damage.

At last Harry came back to us. ''Twill take some time to right it,' he announced. 'Summer Ho is not far—shall we leave it to the men and ride on?'

Sensing his eagerness to be home and glad to be free of the confines of the cumbersome coach, I smiled up at him. 'I'd like it above all things.'

He mounted his horse and edged him nearer me. 'Your foot on my boot, sweetheart,' he instructed and I came into his waiting arms as easily as a bird. For a while I was content to breathe the fresh June air and then began to take an interest in my surroundings, plying my companion with questions.

The steep incline we were climbing led up to Noor Hill, I learned, and ahead lay Summer Ho, Harry's home. At last we topped the hill and Harry stayed the horse, a big black gelding that had carried us both easily. Following his pointing finger, I looked ahead, past his fringed and embroidered gauntlet, past the newly green trees, to where, nestling in a curve of the road a cluster of rose pink buildings stood.

'Home!' said Harry and, hugging me closer,

set Blackboy into a trot.

The wind rushed against my face as we descended the hill. I revelled in our speed and knew a moment's disappointment when we slowed, turned in at the gatehouse and rode through the narrow, short passage beneath it.

And so I saw Summer Ho for the first time, knowing that here, within these walls, would my life be spent. Here would Harry and I live and love and here our children would grow to adulthood. As we passed under the gatehouse and out into the sun-filled courtyard, a sudden chill shook me and Harry held me tighter.

'Cold, my love?' he asked.

I shook my head and was silent. How could I tell him that some vague presentiment of the future had laid its heavy hands on my high spirits and that, for a minute, to my sun-dazzled eyes the house had appeared enveloped in flames.

He blew in my ear, taking my silence for a maidenly nervousness at the prospect of meeting his people. 'Take heart,' he whispered. 'They are none so bad and doubtless eager to meet my bride.'

That was all he had time to say, for at that moment an aged man appeared in the central door which was standing wide, and made haste to descend the shallow steps. Harry reached down and clasped his hand, before sliding to the ground he helped me down from Blackboy's back. One arm round my waist, he swung me round to face the old man.

'Meet your new mistress,' he said. 'Anne, this is Tom Holwell, my steward, but more besides—since my childhood he has stood me in good stead of father and uncles.'

An old, dry hand held mine. 'Welcome, Miss Anne,' he said. Kind blue eyes looked into mine and I knew before I turned away that I would have at least one friend at Summer Ho.

'Come and meet Dame Allis,' Harry urged and, taking my hand, led me up the steps and into the house.

The great hall was dark and, until my eyes became used to the gloom, seemed full of dim, hard to discern shapes. Blinking, I realised that these were servants lined up to receive us and we went slowly down the line. I nodded gravely to the bows and bobs, doing my best to appear blasé and used to such happenings, but in reality my heart sank at the thought of managing so many dependants.

From what I had seen, the house was not too large, but undoubtedly old and inconvenient to run. My father's house had been modern and compact, four stories high as is usual in London and run by my mother's capable hands. Summer Ho had been built in Harry's reign and much added to since—my new life would not be easy, I thought.

While nodding and smiling my way along the servants, my eyes darted into the far, gloomy corners. Doors and corridors seemed to lead off in all directions and I wondered, with a moment's panic, if I would be expected to take over the care of it at once.

'Where is my grandmother?' asked Harry, when we had come to the last of the servants.

'Dame Allis is in the Queen's Chamber,' replied the steward. 'She keeps to her room a great deal nowadays, but I understand that she is planning to come down to dinner this evening.'

By this time the coach had arrived and, as Harry and I climbed the wide staircase, we heard the crunch of its wheels and the shouts of the servants guiding the wagon with our luggage through the gate.

The passage at the top of the stairs was wide and panelled in a dark, linenfold oak. Harry stopped outside a door and scratched at its dark surface. A voice bid us enter and, with an encouraging smile, he lifted the latch and opened the door.

A wave of heat and oppressive air made me pause on the threshold and then Harry's hand urged me forward, while my eyes took in the fact that despite the warm June sun the casements were tight shut and a bright fire burned in the hearth.

The room seemed a blaze of colour. Crimson velvet curtains hung at the mullioned window, gaily embroidered hangings surrounded the fourposter bed, bright carpets covered the floor and on every available surface stood bowls and dishes of glowing Chinese ware.

'Well, Harry, home at last?' said a voice from beside the fire and I turned my fascinated gaze away from the furnishings of the room and looked at the woman who had spoken.

For all her age, she sat fiercely upright, her straight spine a good three inches away from the padded back of her chair. To my surprise she wore the clothes fashionable in the old Queen Elizabeth's days. Embroidered brocade hung in stiff folds to the floor and a high lace ruff rose behind her head and the curls it framed were a bright unbelievable red. I suddenly found that sharp grey eyes were examining me with as much curiosity as I felt and I dropped my gaze in confusion.

'Didn't Harry warn you about me?' she asked abruptly. She touched her skirt. 'I like these fashions better than the namby-pamby colours and styles of today.'

'I was thinking how becoming the ruff is,' I ventured and knew I had chosen aright when I heard a quiet chuckle.

'Come into the light and let me see you,' she said and pulled me to kneel at her feet. One bony hand tilted my chin and the hard eyes stared down into mine. 'You're young,' she said at last, 'and over-worldly I'd say—more interested in dress and finery than housewifely duties.'

'Until now I've had no house to care about—but you'll find that my mother taught

7

me well and that now I have a house, I'm ready to do my duties.'

A wintry smile softened her face for a moment. 'Tch, tch, mind your temper with me,' was all she said, but I could tell she was not unpleased as she released my chin.

'Doubtless she'll prove a goodly wife, Grandson,' she said, looking over my head, and I looked up to find Harry smiling at both of us.

He came forward and rested one hand on my shoulder. 'Doubtless she will—an you don't bully her too much.'

The drop pearls on her lace cap trembled as she looked down at me. 'Methinks we'll have an understanding,' she answered. 'After all we both have the same objective—to do our best for Summer Ho and all within its walls. Pray God the coming times treat us kindly. What news of the King when you left London?'

She gave me a little push towards a stool at her feet and I sat down as Harry began to speak.

'Nothing new—the King still wanders the countryside. You know he left London after his raid on the House of Commons and went first to Hampton Court. I believe he is now in York trying to rally the gentlemen there and forming a bodyguard.'

'I fear there will be trouble.' She sighed and touched one finger to her thin mouth. 'I fear there will be civil war. I've heard tales of the old

8

troubles between the Roses from my grandfather. Civil strife is the worst that can befall a country. Brother fights brother and father kills child, while we women sit at home and pray for our menfolk.'

'Surely, ma'am, it will not come to that?' I cried. Her words had made the possibility more real to me than all my father's head shakings and ill-printed news sheets.

'No man would dare strike at the King,' comforted my husband. 'It will all come to naught and the men from Parliament will slink home with their tails between their legs.'

'Pray Heaven 'tis so,' murmured his grandmother and, for a moment, all was silent in the room, each of us busy with our own troubled thoughts; then Dame Allis shook herself, setting her jewels aquiver and seemed determined to put off such dull thoughts. 'Away with you,' she commanded. 'If I am to dine in the great hall, I need my rest. I grow old, Harry, and my bones feel tired.'

At once he came to her and lifted her hand to his lips. 'Madam,' he said, bowing gracefully, 'You'll never grow old—you are forever young.'

For a moment I thought she would take affront at such arrant flattery, but saw that her eyes had softened and she was pleased. Her free hand reached out and lightly touched the fair hair so near her, but all she said was, 'Away, and take your lady with you.'

9

I rose hastily and dropped her a curtsey, but she took no notice and I saw her eyes were dull and her thoughts elsewhere.

By the time Harry had shown me to our room, the trunks had been carried upstairs and Meg was unpacking them. She turned as I entered and smiled over the top of a pile of linen.

'Oh, Miss, such a big old house 'tis,' she exclaimed, 'not new like the one you've left. The kitchen's miles away ... the water will be cold before it gets here.'

''Tis the price we must pay for antiquity,' I answered lightly. 'I believe parts of the house date from the fifteenth century.' I looked around thoughtfully. 'I believe that I shall find such age interesting.'

'Well, now you've married into the nobility 'tis only right,' Meg pointed out, 'but me—I'd prefer the modern merchant's comforts.'

A few days ago and I would have agreed with her, but already the atmosphere of the old house had begun to attract me. I went to the mullioned window and looked out. My room was above the great hall and looked onto the courtyard. Almost opposite was the gate house with its narrow entrance and small room above for the guard so necessary for protecting the house in the troubled times when it was built. Running my hand over the smooth wood of the windowseat, I idly wondered at the history of Summer Ho and, my husband entering at that

10

moment, I asked him for information.

He shrugged. 'You'll have to ask the Dame. I've never bothered with things past. Old, dry happenings mean nothing to a man. 'Tis life and living that matter to me.'

I was to remember his words much later, but then I only noticed his arm sliding round my waist and his nod of dismissal to Meg. Obediently she put down the pile of dresses she was carrying and moved towards the door. Reluctantly I slipped out of his grasp and called to her.

'Don't go—we have much to do before we dine.' I turned to Harry and smiled apologetically. ''Twould never do to keep Dame Allis waiting.'

'Perhaps you are right,' he agreed and walked across the room, his spurs clinking on the wooden boards. At the door he looked back and grinned meaningly at me over the top of Meg's head. 'You'll find that we keep country hours here, sweetheart. We sup early ... and bed early.'

As the door closed behind him, I felt a rosy blush rise under Meg's knowing eyes. 'A bath,' I said quickly before she could say anything. 'I feel the need to remove the dust of travel. Quickly, girl, order it for me and we'll test the truth of your prophecy of cold water.'

Having been with me since we were both children, Meg is a little forward at times and I have to show her who is the mistress. I watched

11

her skirt flick round the corner of the door and then sank down upon the bed. Although well-proportioned the room was none so grand as the one Dame Allis occupied and I began to realise that she held a very special place at Summer Ho. For a moment I toyed with the idea of trying to usurp it, but, quickly realising that it would prove almost impossible, decided that to win her friendship was more realistic . . . and more within my powers. Dame Allis might be old and, from what Harry said I believed her almost in her eightieth year, but she still had all her faculties and, from the little I had seen of her, I knew that her will was still as strong as it had ever been. Doubtless, from the very nature of our characters, she and I would cross swords more than once, but I had a feeling that there might be friendship between us, too.

CHAPTER TWO

A few days later, when I had begun to feel at home at Summer Ho, Harry suggested that we ride out together to inspect the estate. Nothing loath, I changed into my riding habit and ran to join him in the hall.

Conscious of looking my best in the tawny coloured velvet, I was pleased to see the blaze of admiration in his eyes as he turned and saw me. Swiftly he came to the foot of the stairs and, clasping his hands round my waist, lifted me down the last few steps. For a breathless second he held me in the air, my hands on his shoulders and then allowed me to slide down until I was firmly caught against his chest.

'A forfeit, sweetheart,' he demanded in my ear and I raised my face for his kiss, before disentangling myself and running out into the courtyard.

A groom waited there with Blackboy and a little grey mare. Although small, she was beautifully made and pranced prettily on her delicate hooves.

'What a sweet creature,' I exclaimed.

''Tis yours,' said Harry. 'My present to you—you have need of a mount and when I saw her some weeks ago, I knew she was the right weight for you.'

I took the reins and, pulling the grey head down to me, smoothed the velvety muzzle. She resisted at first until I blew gently into her nostrils and then she grew quiet and leaned against my shoulder.

'We shall be friends,' I said and turned to Harry to ask her name. 'Mab,' he answered. 'And surely fitting for so dainty and fairylike an animal.'

'Doubtless we'll fly over many a hedge together,' I laughed as he cupped his hands for my foot and threw me into the saddle.

For all the day was young and wanting several hours to noon, the sun was warm with

13

promise of great heat to come. We clattered over the cobbles and left the courtyard by means of a gate set in a corner next to the stables.

'We'll see the park first,' Harry explained, seeing my puzzled look, for I had expected to leave by the gatehouse.

We passed the Tudor gardens on the other side of the house and skirted the vegetable gardens, then let out our horses across the soft undulating parkland dotted with oaks that had been planted a hundred years before, when the house was being rebuilt.

Mab was well named for indeed she flew like the fairy queen herself. Blackboy, for all his great strength and stride, had difficulty keeping level with her.

'We could beat you an we really wanted to,' I challenged when at last we drew rein under one of the trees.

'On a short run, but over distance stamina would tell,' said Harry who would allow no disparagement of his favourite mount.

'One day we will see,' I said 'but not until I know her better.' I patted her neck and looked around. 'Where now?' I asked.

'The Home Farm—I have business there and then we'll join the road and ride home more circumspectly.'

As I had expected, the Home Farm had all the signs of being prosperous, lying snug and neat in a hollow of the land amid open

14

meadows. A rough track led up to it and we joined it where a barred gate bisected the road. At Harry's shout the door flew open and a girl ran out, her face bright with welcome. At sight of me she stopped, while the smile faded from her lips. Then slowly, deliberately, she sauntered to the gate and opened it. I looked at Harry to see what he would make of such insolence and found him watching the girl with a slow smile in his eyes. As we rode into the farmyard he reached out of the saddle and flicked her lightly with the tip of his whip.

'Take care you serve me quicker next time,' he said.

Something in his tone disturbed me and I looked back over my shoulder in time to see the girl bob her head to hide a smile as she closed the gate. I turned to Harry again but, at that moment, the farmer came out of the house closely followed by his stout wife and I was distracted by introductions.

'And ... this is your daughter?' I asked when they had done with bowings and bobbings.

'One of 'em, mistress,' answered the farmer 'for we have been blessed with a quiverful of girls and but one boy. Betty is our eldest.'

I smiled as she curtsied and searched her face anew but, apart from a fleeting glance at me, she kept her eyes lowered and I could not guess at her thoughts. I imagined her about sixteen but, well built and bonny, she could have been older. Golden curls spilled out from under her

15

confining cap and her glowing country colour showed to advantage against its snowy whiteness.

'You'll take a cup of ale, mistress?' suggested the farmer's wife.

'Yes, do,' said Harry, turning for a moment from his conversation. 'I have much to discuss and will be some time. Do you go in with Goodie Green.'

The kitchen was overhot with a fire burning on the hearth. A savoury smell arose from the cooking pot hanging over it, mingling its odour with the onions, bacon and bunches of herbs dangling from the ceiling. A babe mewed in its cradle by the fire and, on the brick floor, a cat and her kittens ignored the hens and chicks that ran in at the open door. The only chair was placed for me and I drew off my gloves as the goodwife set a mug of ale on the table beside me.

'You have a healthy family,' I complimented her, smiling at the children who peered solemnly at me. 'Are they usually so silent?'

'Noisy as a herd of pigs,' she answered cheerfully, 'but that's how I'd have 'em, then I know nothing ails them.'

'How many have you?'

'The new babe makes six,' she paused and added with justifiable pride, 'only two have I lost ... and they was just little mites. Not so bad then,' she explained. 'Not so fond of 'em then, see.'

A movement at the door caught my attention and I looked to see the girl, Betty sidling into the room. Her mother gestured to her to be gone but I put out a detaining hand.

'Let her come ... an she will. Come here, girl,' I said and motioned her to come forward. 'Have you something to say to me? I have seen you looking at me.'

She shook her head and twisted on her thick brogues.

'What, then?' I asked firmly.

''Tis nothing,' she answered sullenly.

I looked at the goodwife who was watching silently and she came forward to put one hand on her daughter's shoulder. Fingers gripping hard, she smiled at me and said, 'The girl is shy, mistress—if you'd allow me, I'd say she wants to see your clothes. Never seen a fine lady before, has my Bet.'

And with that I had to be content though I would swear that it was not shyness that held the girl's tongue. Soon after we left the farm and I put the matter out of my head. Summer Ho and its inhabitants claimed all my attention. Gradually I came to know all its rooms and treasures. I turned to Dame Allis for stories of its past and discovered an unexpected interest in history. The old woman was a born raconteur and made her tales live for me, not like the dry as dust, pedantic speech of my tutor as he recounted happenings of the ancient Greeks and Romans. Dame Allis and I had found a mutual interest and I spent many hours in her chamber, crouched on a stool at her knee.

Her stories were fascinating relics of a more bawdy age and I found delight in her free treatment of me as a woman. As a Lady-in-waiting to the old Queen, she knew many risqué tales of the Elizabethan court and entertained both Harry and me for many an evening.

One day after dinner, she recounted a more riotous tale than usual concerning Sir Walter Raleigh. 'Now Sir Walter,' she said, 'ever had an eye for a pretty wench and this particular evening had managed to waylay a Lady-in-waiting, who shall be nameless. So quick were his advances and so great her confusion that her protests quickly passed from "Sweet Sir Walter" to "Swisser Swasser, Swisser Swasser!"' The old woman held up her hands and tilted back her hand to enjoy her laughter. Her standing collar shook and her outrageous wig slipped a little askew, until a lock of grey hair appeared to my fascinated eyes.

Wiping her eyes on a rich handkerchief, she reached up and flicked the errant headpiece back in place with a careless tap. 'Ah me,' she sighed. 'The Court was somewhere for enjoyment then, not a dull place interested only in the arts and a friendly kiss frowned upon as it is now. The old Queen, now there was a Monarch! None could doubt her royal blood and every inch of her regal, but she lived every minute and the people could believe her one of them. She had the common touch—and was proud of it.'

'You were fond of her?'

The old eyes looked at me. 'Fond?' she repeated on an inquiring note. 'I loved her. Not because she was Queen and it was my duty, but for herself. She was stubborn and a tyrant. She had a vicious tongue that would have put a fishwife to shame and yet I loved her ... perhaps because I could see her faults ... and knew she had much to account for her trying ways.'

'She stayed here, at Summer Ho?'

'Soon after I was married. She was on a Progress and broke her journeying here, sleeping in this very room, which was furnished for her.' She looked lovingly around the walls and hangings. 'I worked the furnishings myself during my betrothal.'

'They are very fine.'

'You'll find none like them nowadays. The modern woman has no knowledge of real needlework. 'Tis all this "stumpwork" and finicky little pictures, not something that would take years to finish. No backbone, the young woman of today.'

'Anne has a very pretty backbone, as I can vow,' put in Harry wickedly, and his grandmother cackled with delight. He rose and stretched his long legs in front of the fire, looking down at us both with a smile. 'But you are wrong, madam,' he said. 'The Court might be dull—on the surface, but underneath! If my wife wasn't here such tales as I could tell!'

'Tch, tch,' said the old woman impatiently. 'I'll not believe that His Majesty has a thought in his head but that bigoted Catholic he married.'

'He has eyes for no-one else,' agreed Harry.

'And there lies trouble. If I mistake me not she holds too much power.'

I sighed and let their conversation drift over my head, having no interest in politics, or the King whom I had never seen. Everyone I knew had great interest in the political situation, but I regarded such things for the old and staid, or for men. Lighter, more exciting matters occupied my mind. A dinner at Summer Ho had been talked of and there were still the "Bride Visits" to pay to the local gentry. Now that I was more settled in my position, such visits would be expected of me, I knew, but as it happened neither the dinner nor the visits took place.

I was woken from my reverie by the sound of swift approaching horse hooves. For a moment we all looked at each other wondering who could be out so late at night, for the moon was overcast and made travelling difficult. Then Harry lifted his shoulders from the fireplace and went to the window.

Silently I followed him and watched as a

horseman rode under the gatehouse and clattered across the cobbles to be met at the steps by Steward Holwell. A torch flared and illuminated his face beneath the wide brimmed hat.

Harry sucked in a breath. ''Tis Ashley Death,' he exclaimed. 'He promised to bring news if...' leaving the sentence unfinished he swung round and left the room, leaving Dame Allis and me alone.

'What can it be?' I asked, but already a feeling of dread had begun to seize me.

The old woman pursed her lips and shook her head. 'Best go and find out girl,' she advised. 'My curiosity grows and fain would I find out what is happening.'

I stopped at the door. 'I'll tell you, never fear,' I assured her before closing the door behind me.

Heels tapped impatiently, I ran along the passages and down the stairs, pausing as I saw my husband below in conversation with the mysterious rider. Shadows danced across the great hall as the candles flared in the draught from the open door and both men looked up as I slowly descended the stairs.

The stranger's eyes flickered over me and he stepped forward sweeping his feathered hat from his head in a gallant manner. 'Pray present me, Harry,' he said.

'Sir Ashley Death—Mistress Anne, my wife,' said Harry and reluctantly I put my fingers into the outstretched hand.

Why I should feel so, I had no idea. The man bowing before me was handsome and obviously prepared to be friendly, but there was a cool certainty about him, a sureness that I would be charmed by him, that I could not like. Self-possessed, with an unhidden arrogance, he looked deeply into my eyes and waited for my heart to flutter—as doubtless so many other female hearts had fluttered under his almost animal magnetism.

'My pleasure, sir,' I said gravely and, withdrawing my hand, went to my husband's side. 'You said something of news—your Grandmother and I are anxious.'

'You have reason ... Sir Ashley brings word that there has been a skirmish at Manchester and that His Majesty is setting up his standard at Nottingham. He is calling all loyal men to his side.'

My heart, which had been beating quickly, suddenly slowed and knocked against my ribs. 'You'll go?' I asked needlessly through dry lips.

'I must declare myself,' he answered gravely, but I saw the gleam of excitement in his eyes. Seeing the expression on my face, he seized my hands and held them tightly. 'You would not have me turn traitor?' he asked. 'We'll soon show these damned Parliament men their places and be home again. Sweetheart, you would not have me stay safe at home while others fight for their King?'

22

'Have no fear, mistress,' put in Ashley Death. ''Twill soon be over and, until then, I promise to watch over him like a guardian angel.'

I summoned up a smile and turned again to the stairs. 'I'll tell Dame Allis. She charged me to dispel her curiosity.' I paused at the bend in the stairs and, looking back, saw the two men deep in conversation with their heads close together, and knew that I was already forgot. For all their talk of loyalty, I knew that it was really the thought of adventure that spurred them. I was young enough to know envy and feel a wish to accompany them on their ride northwards. To ride away on a chivalrous venture was excitement, but to stay at home and play a woman's part I found was not to my liking. Remembering the old romances I had heard, I half contemplated the possibility of donning breeches and leaving in their trail. By the time I reached the Queen's Chamber, I had almost convinced myself of the adventure ahead and, torn between fear and excitement, opened the door declaring, ''Tis an end of shilly-shallying. The King has set up his standard and calls all loyal gentlemen to him. Harry will join him … and I wish with all my heart that I might ride out as well!'

CHAPTER THREE

During the next few days all was hustle at Summer Ho. Getting Harry ready to ride to Nottingham, I saw little of him, being much occupied in sorting his linen and clothes. He spent many hours closeted with Ashley Death and, closer knowledge of that gentleman, did nothing to dispel my first impression of him but to my husband he could obviously do no wrong.

As many men as could be spared were to ride with Harry and he was taking his own servant with him. This would leave us with a sadly depleted force but as yet, there was no sign of trouble in Hampshire, he felt justified in leaving us so.

Having assured him that I was a match for any number of rebels and that his grandmother and I would defend Summer Ho to the last drop of our blood, I set to my tasks with a will as the day proposed for their departure approached.

The evening before they were to leave, we all dined together, being honoured by the presence of Dame Allis, who seemed much taken with Sir Ashley. Never had I seen her so animated and rarely before or since, seen such a display of jewels as she carried about her.

Good wax candles lit the damask and silver

on the table, the casements stood wide to catch a breeze that carried the scents of flowers into the room. The scene seemed so peaceful, so ordinary that I found it hard to believe that tomorrow the men beside me would ride away to war.

At last the tablecloth was taken away and nuts and wine placed on the polished boards. I think that I shall always remember the picture the others made; the golden candle glow lit Harry's face and fair hair as he turned laughing to the man beside him, while Ashley Death leaned one arm on the table, his dark satanic features alight with amusement at their shared joke. Behind them Dame Allis watched, her face ageless and inscrutable.

Suddenly the trivial conversation, when tomorrow Harry would ride away to danger, the laughter and atmosphere heavy with wine and tobacco, became too much to be born and, muttering my excuses, I slipped away, hoping I was unseen. The garden was cool and sweet after the overheated air of the dining room and, for a while, I walked aimlessly, discovering a soothing delight in the black shadows and cold moonlight. Sitting beside the pond, I idly watched the ripples chasing each other across its smooth surface. Busy with myriads of thoughts, I lost all sense of time and had just realised that I was becoming chilled, when a movement in the shadows drew my attention and I saw that someone was watching me. At my involuntary start the figure came forward and I recognised Ashley.

'Are you lost, sir?' I asked coldly, not liking the idea of being spied upon.

'No, mistress—merely not wishing to break the spell of beauty you cast upon this spot!'

What woman can resist flattery? I own no immunity and it was in a kinder tone that I asked him what he would.

'Harry grows anxious. He fears you will take a chill in the night air.' He reached a hand to help me to my feet and, as I raised my eyebrows in mute question, explained, 'He is playing backgammon with his grandmother ... and, besides, he knows I desire to make your better acquaintance.'

Deliberately ignoring the meaning hidden in his voice, I pulled my fingers from his grasp, saying lightly, 'You were not at our wedding, I think. I have no recollection of seeing you there.'

'An I had been you'd not have forgotten so soon.'

Darting him a swift glance under my lashes, I saw his teeth gleam and knew that he was laughing at me. 'How so? Methinks a Bride's attention would be taken up by her Groom.'

'So convention would have us believe,' his voice was bland. 'I could have wished to be there, but I was in France, visiting my mother's relations.'

'Your mother is French? Then that would

account for—' I broke off in some confusion; dislike him as I might, I could hardly be rude to my husband's friend.

'For my looks—or my manners?' he asked and I heard the amusement in his voice.

'Oh, I believe the French are quite civilised!' I said outrageously.

For a moment there was silence and into the quiet night an owl hooted somewhere near. The man beside me laid hands on my shoulders and turned me into the moonlight. I stared up as his dark eyes searched my face. When, at last, he spoke his voice was serious, all amusement gone.

'I believe, Mistress Anne, that you bear me little love.'

'You are my husband's friend.'

'That is no answer ... what reason have you to hold me in dislike?'

When I would have looked away, his fingers tilted up my chin so that I must perforce meet those black eyes again. Finding this new side of him confusing, I bit my lip and said what I thought.

'If you must know, sir, I neither like nor dislike, but rather am indifferent to you. I am a merchant's daughter and doubtless have different values to you, but to spend your time in endless visits to kinsmen, in wild carousing, in meetings with your friends, in drinking and gaming and more—of which, being a female I'm supposed to know nothing—seems a great

27

waste to me.'

He let me go and turned away, speaking more to himself than to me. 'And you have learned all this of me in such a short time?'

'You are too sure that all women will find your charm attractive,' I added harshly to his back.

'Ah!' he swung around. 'You are angry because I flirted with you.' Coming close, but not touching me, he went on quickly, 'Thank Heaven, madam, that you are Harry's wife ... or I would have made you love me.'

A thousand emotions rose in me, anger that he should suppose me so easily won, and indignation at his perfidy foremost among them but, before I could find words to express my feelings, my hand was taken and drawn through Sir Ashley's arm to lie snug in the crook of his elbow.

'The hour grows late,' he said coolly, 'shall we go in?' and for a moment I could almost believe that I had imagined his previous statement, but then I looked up and saw his dark eyes gleaming down at me and, reading the cynical amusement in their depths, knew that I'd heard aright.

My hand sought for release, but his grip was firm and his face implacable and, realising the indignity of fighting for my freedom, I relaxed and allowed him to lead me across the lawn towards the house. On the shallow steps he paused and, looking down at me said,

'We'd best call a truce, madam.'

'As you will,' I answered striving for indifference.

''Tis neither the time or place—but circumstances alter, mistress, and when they do, be sure I will be ready to resume our ... conversation.' Taking my hand from his arm, he carried it to his lips and then led me up the steps and into the house.

Sleep was hard to find that night and, at last, I climbed out of the big bed and, leaving Harry sleeping like a babe, walked across the cold floor to the window and sat on the windowseat. The country outside was grey and dark. Still and motionless in the night air, the familiar view seemed strangely different and I could almost believe that a unicorn would wander out from the trees and stand, milk white and enchanted, under my window. When something did move below, I sucked in my breath quickly but saw at once that it was no character from a fairy tale, but a being of flesh and blood.

Drawing back into the shadow of the curtain, I watched as Ashley Death walked across the gravel path beneath my window. Head bent in thought, he passed quickly from view and I wrinkled my nose at the pungent scent of tobacco that he left behind. Knowing that his rest was troubled brought a little triumphant relief to me, but, against my wish, I wondered what kept him from his bed. Could it be remembrance of our conversation, that so bothered me, or thoughts of the coming journey and all that it might bring?

I closed my eyes against the thought of battle, but against my will, the clash of sword against steel and the cries of wounded men seemed to echo about the silent room. Circumstances alter, Ashley had said. What if Harry was killed? I looked across to the sleeping man and, with a smothered cry, ran over the wooden boards to him and climbed up into the high soft bed. Harry murmured and drew me close to his side. Holding him tightly I buried my head in his shoulder and waited for the night to end.

I must have slept at last, for when I awoke I found the sun streaming in at the window and the place beside me empty. Quickly sitting up, I saw Harry pulling on his clothes. He smiled when he saw I was awake and came to sit on the bed beside me.

'You were sleeping so prettily that I hadn't the heart to wake you.'

'I wish you had—we have so little time together.'

'We'll be back before autumn arrives, you'll see,' he said confidently and bent to pull on his lacetopped boothose.

'I wish Ashley Death had never come!'

He looked up. 'Nay—never say so, sweetheart. He is my good friend and we've ridden on many an adventure together. He was my first friend at school and we went on the Grand Tour together. Ashley is like a brother to me. At one time we thought that he and Letty would make a match of it.' His face clouded. 'But it came to naught ... Denzil Halt came along and offered for her. There's no denying he had the better fortune and I suppose she fancied a house in the Midlands, but I wish she'd taken Ashley.'

I stared at him in surprise. 'Your sister chose her own husband?' I asked incredulously. 'But surely you and Dame Allis had a say in the matter?'

Harry laughed. 'You don't know Letty. She seems the softest, most guileless creature imaginable, but somehow she always gets her own way. Even as children she always had the biggest apple or the choicest sweetmeat.' He stood up and pulled back the bedclothes. 'Time to rise, my love, if you've a mind to flutter your handkerchief to us.'

And so the war that was to last so many years began for me and, who could guess that that bright June morning was the beginning of so dark and dangerous a time for us all. I remember how the sun warmed my back as I stood on the steps and watched the men mount their horses. Harry rode his Blackboy and Ashley was on a lively chestnut. With their gay clothes, bright sashes and long hair under the broad rimmed hats, they looked like a picture from a masque or one of Master Shakespeare's plays.

A touch at my elbow recalled me to my surroundings and there was good Tom Holwell with a tray bearing the stirrup cups. I looked at Dame Allis who had come out onto the doorway with me. Her eyes met mine over the top of her fur edged cloak, for she was well wrapped even on such a morning and she smiled.

'You take it round, child. My legs grow old and ... besides 'tis your place.'

Harry bent from the saddle and took a cup in his gloved hand. He held it to my lips and when I had sipped, he put his mouth to the place I had touched and drained the warm liquid. I stared up at him wordlessly, the sun in my eyes so that I could only see him as a black silhouette against the blue sky and then I turned and offered the tray to Sir Ashley.

Soon there was nothing more to be done, nothing to delay them any longer. The horses were fidgeting and eager to be gone and the men impatient to begin their journey. Although farewells had been said, I ran to Harry and, with one foot on his boot where it rested in his stirrup, I reached up for his kiss. He held me to him in a bear hug and kissed me soundly, then looked into my face.

'Why so sad, sweetheart? Such a long face is an ill memory to take with me.'

Before I could reply, Ashley's cool voice came over my shoulder and I knew a momentary surprise that he could understand how I felt.

'We are the ones who ride away, Harry—our women folk must sit at home and wait for news. Suspense is never so joyful as action, I'll wager.'

I looked at him as Harry set me back on my feet. 'I had not suspected you of so much perception,' I said slowly.

'I'll give you my word that we'll send you a message whenever possible,' he said and leaned from the saddle to take my hand in his warm grasp, before, pulling on his gauntleted gloves, he gathered the reins into his hands and led the way across the cobbled yard towards the gatehouse.

They looked back once before finally turning onto the road and lifted their arms in salute as they vanished under the dark archway. I listened to the horse hooves for a few seconds before turning away. A hand touched my shoulder and I looked up to see that Dame Allis had waited after the others had gone.

''Tis best to think of something to occupy us,' she said. 'Busy hands will keep our minds from sad thoughts. Let us go into the stillroom and make an inventory of what needs replacing this summer.'

But as it happened, we had no need to busy ourselves with such mundane matters; we had only been in the stillroom a few minutes when

33

Meg came in with a rush of excitement and bobbed a quick curtsey.

'A coach and riders do be coming into the yard, mistress,' she cried. 'Master Holwell sent me to say that he thinks 'tis Lord Halt's arms upon the side.'

'Lettice!' exclaimed Dame Allis. 'Doubtless they'll have heard the news and Denzil is bringing her here for safety, while he rides to the King.' She stood up and shook out the folds of her wide skirt. 'We must meet them and make them welcome.' She smiled at me. 'I'll wager you'll find your sister Lettice a good distraction from your worries.'

I was all eagerness to meet this unknown sister of Harry's, but I must own to a little disappointment when I first saw her. What I had expected, I don't quite know, perhaps a female counterpart of my husband. Certainly not this pretty blonde creature that was fluttering like a bird on her husband's arm when I arrived in the hall.

'I vow I am fatigued to death,' she was saying, clinging to him and drooping prettily. 'The journey was too much for me—I must lie down before I swoon away.'

'Good day, Letty—you look well,' put in Dame Allis receiving her kiss. 'And you, Denzil, how are you?'

A pair of blue eyes were turned in my direction and swept me from head to foot, before her high sweet voice cooed, 'And this

34

must be Harry's wife. I swear I've been longing these months to meet my new sister.'

A soft cheek touched mine and I was engulfed in a cloud of perfume. Lettice Halt was several inches higher than I but contrived to give the impression that she had to stand on a tiptoe to reach me. All my life I had cursed my own lack of inches, but I was to learn that my sister-in-law played willingly on her own supposed lack of height. Acting to perfection the dainty, little woman weak and frail, who must ever be consulted and waited upon ... and such was the charm that she could exude that we all did so willingly.

Dame Allis proved right when she suggested that Lettice would distract me from my worries. Letty took a liking to me and vowing friendship and sisterly love, kept me by her side most of the time when I was free from my housewifely duties. Her main interests seemed to be fashion and dress and gossip about various members of the family or famous people. Her artless chatter and irresponsible views filled me with amusement which I was careful to conceal. Never having met anyone like her before I found her fascinating and, while I could not like her, danced attendance on her like a bedazzled moth, blinded for the moment by her knowledgeable ways and pretty looks.

After a few days, Denzil Halt rode north and the inmates of Summer Ho settled down to await news of their menfolk. The weather was warm and life went on as usual in any great house. Plants flowered and bushes fruited. I found an unexpected delight in restocking the stillroom. Preserves and jam were made, the heavy copper pans in the kitchen were never empty and soon a new joy, which I had suspected, became a certainty. I hugged it to myself at first, secretly cherishing it in my bosom until one day, catching a speculative look in Dame Allis' shrewd eyes, I could keep it secret no longer.

CHAPTER FOUR

The summer passed quickly, we learned that Harry and Ashley Death had joined the brigade of the King's nephew, Prince Rupert at Nottingham. The Prince had been a soldier since his teens and Harry was full of enthusiasm for his skill and leadership. Lord Halt offered his staider services to His Majesty's own troop. Our first victory came in September, when Harry and Ashley charged under Rupert's command and the Royalists took Powick Bridge in Worcestershire.

We lived in dread for the next message from the battlefield, but when it came I was not in the house to receive it. The weather was fine for late October and, unable to ride my mare because of my condition, I was walking in the park at some distance from the house, when Letty sent Meg to find me.

'A message!' I gasped, repeating her words as my heart began to bump inside my bodice.

'From the master for sure,' she said comfortingly. 'The fellow had no long face about him as he would've for certain if it had been bad news. No need to hurry so,' she went on as I began walking back to the house, 'he's in the kitchen, behind a big tankard of ale and looks as if he'll never move again.'

So I found him when, at last, I burst into the kitchen. He was seated at the table, with an excited gaggle of maidservants hanging upon his every word and an interesting looking bandage about his head. Wiping his mouth on the back of his hand, he stood up at my approach and, fumbling in his pocket, held out a bulky package to me.

'The Lieutenant said as you'd give me a night's lodgings.'

'Of course—you can find a place in the stables,' I answered impatiently, 'but what of my husband? Is he well?'

He grinned. 'Aye ... and a sight better than a good few of the Roundheads he met at Edgehill Ridge.'

'You've—been in battle?'

Again he grinned and nodded slowly. 'Aye—twice. I'm in the Captain's—Captain Death's troop and if'n I hadn't been knocked on the head by a Rebel's pike, I'd be there still. Sent me home, the Captain has, until I'm better like and Lieutenant Summer asked me to bring you the letters on the way.'

'My thanks. Sit down and eat your fill. Come to me in the morning before you leave and I'll reward you for your trouble.' I whisked out of the room, eager to read the letter Harry had sent me. Dame Allis and Letty were waiting impatiently in the hall and the latter pounced on me as I appeared.

'What news?' asked the Dame quietly, not moving from her seat by the fire.

'Did he bring nothing for me? I vow I feel strangely neglected. Denzil should think of me more. Once when we were parted, be it never so short a time, he'd send me little reminders and remembrances each day, but now 'tis more than a month since I heard of him and that was the curtest note.'

By this time I had undone the outer paper and found enclosed two smaller packets. One addressed in Lord Halt's small neat handwriting, I handed to Letty without a word and the other dropped into Dame Allis' lap, then moved nearer the fire to read my own closely written outer sheet.

My eyes skimmed down Harry's bold, black script, not staying to decipher the whole, just gathering the gist of the letter, but when I returned to the top to begin again, the older woman's voice broke in upon me.

'An it's not too personal, read it to us, Anne. Harry has sent me a button from the coat of a captured Parliament man ... but no news.'

'His Royal Majesty,' I read aloud, 'has had the most joyous victory. The Royal camp is jubilant and the Parliamentarians slink away like whipped curs.

'It was this wise; the Rhinish Prince and his troop, of whom you know Ashley and I number, bypassed Worcester where Essex and his men lay and occupied the ridge above Edgehill near Kineton. Meanwhile the King, who had ridden from the west, turned on his pursuers and attacked before their rearguard had come up from Kineton village. The Prince charged the Parliamentarians' horse and then pursued them and plundered the baggage train, which you must know is considered honourable and a part of warfare.

'Seeing Hampton and his men approaching, we rode back to the field and gave much needed aid to the King's infantry which had withstood the Rebels' foot soldiers and several bodies of horse.

''Tis said that many were saved that fell wounded by reason of the extreme cold that prevailed all that night and so sealed up their wounds and stopped their blood. I escaped unhurt, but Ashley was gashed upon the face by an enemy pike. He says 'tis only his beauty that is spoiled, and I fear that he will now afright all the ladies that once looked upon him so kindly.

'My duties to your own self and my grandmother. Pray give the fellow that brought this a shilling for his troubles and take heart that I will hasten to return to you whenever His Majesty has no further use for my services.'

'By God's teeth!' burst out the old lady when I had finished. 'I've never known Harry to write at such length. Wielding a sword must be good exercise for his pen. And what says my Lord Halt?'

Letty sniffed. 'Little enough. Much about the battle which you know already and I can hardly understand, there is so much of tactics and orders about it, and precious little else. He never once asks after me and seems more concerned that I should send him his heavy cloak as the nights are cold and he thought to be home before he should have need of it.'

'And is that all?' I asked.

'Well, he does say that 'tis rumoured that the King will head for Oxford and intends to winter there.'

'Oxford ... but 'tis not so far away surely?' I burst out, having but a hazy idea of geography. 'Mayhap he and Harry will be home soon.'

And so it proved to be. One dull day in late November I was reading to Dame Allis in the Queen's Chamber and sitting by the window to catch the last of the afternoon light. My hands were chilled with cold and I had just put the

40

book by while I chafed some warmth into them when, happening to glance up, I saw a little troop of horsemen riding down the hill toward Summer Ho. Not wishing to alarm Dame Allis I said nothing, while trying to make out whether they were friends or no, but something in my manner must have warned her, for she suddenly called out,

'What is it? What have you seen, girl?'

'Horsemen,' I was forced to answer, as she left her chair and came to stand behind me, 'but a small band and nothing to fear, I'm sure.'

We stood together straining our eyes through the gathering dusk, then a hatbrim lifted, black hair fluttered in the wind and I recognised Ashley Death and beside him, my husband.

''Tis Harry!' I cried excitedly to the Dame and on the words turned and hurried out of the room, down the dark stairs and into the hall, calling for Tom the steward as I went. Only stopping to acquaint him with the news and set such orders as necessary into motion, I flung open the heavy front door and ran out onto the steps, just as the cavalcade of horsemen rode under the gatehouse.

The damp wind lifted my skirts as Harry dropped from his mount and we met in a fierce embrace at the foot of the steps.

'Welcome, oh, welcome home!' I cried and felt his arms close tightly about me.

41

Almost at once he released his grasp and, setting me away from him, said, 'How now, sweeting?' His eyes ran over me and I saw enlightenment dawn in them. ''Tis a rotund little wife that greets me—how say you, Ashley?'

I felt his friend's gaze upon me and knew a flush rose to cover my cheeks at his scrutiny.

'I'd say ... that never have I seen Mistress Anne so blooming,' he said quietly and bowed over my hand.

Harry laughed and put an arm around my shoulders as we went indoors. 'A little weight becomes you, my love,' he whispered. 'So I am to be a father—when do you expect the babe?'

'In March,' I answered. 'Say you can stay that long.'

He made no answer but into the silence, Ashley said, 'Doubtless something can be arranged.'

'The King has need ...' Harry began, but a voice cut across his words.

'The King can wait, 'tis your wife will need you at such a time.' And we all turned to see Dame Allis at the foot of the stairs.

'Well, Harry, I'm glad to see you—and you, Sir Ashley,' she said, coming forward. 'You've given us many anxious moments.'

'Is my lord with you?' cried Letty from the shadows as, aroused by the noise, she arrived from her chamber. 'No, Denzil has gone on to Oxford with His Majesty, but he has sent a bolt of cloth for you. My man will bring it in anon.'

We all gathered around the huge fireplace in the hall, while Master Holwell served hot punch. The little pewter cup was hot to my hand and I closed my chilled fingers around it with enjoyment. Now I could look at my husband unobserved and could see little change in him, for all his first experience of warfare. He was a little thinner, but his hair glowed as brightly as ever in the firelight. A movement beside him caught my attention and I found myself gazing at Ashley Death and, intrigued, I found him much changed. Always slim, his leanness now gave hint of the hard muscles underneath. The flickering light showed new lines about his eyes and mouth and, across one cheek a vivid scar drew a brilliant line.

Closing my eyes at the thought of the fierce fight that had caused it, I opened them to find him beside me. 'Will it mar my looks?' he asked, disdaining any subterfuge.

''Tis scarcely noticeable...' I began and, stopped by his frowning look, went on more truthfully. 'It is very new yet, but will doubtless fade in time.' I studied him more closely. 'I believe that many will find it attractive ... indeed it gives you a look of one of Drake's wild buccaneers that is not unbecoming.'

He smiled down at me, but not before I had seen the momentary relief in his eyes and suddenly I wondered, if for the first time in his life, this man had been unsure of himself. If he

43

had been, the feeling soon passed, or I had been most reassuring, for in the days that followed he gave no sign of being conscious of his spoiled face, giving the impression of even more assurance than ever.

He and Harry were ever in each other's company. They filled our larder with the spoils of their hunting and, when the nearby woods were empty, rode further afield until the sport palled and they turned to new pastimes, spending hours in gaming and drinking.

Denzil Halt came home for Christmas and the holiday came and went. We tried to make the most of it, but somehow an air of tenseness hung over the house despite all Dame Allis and I could do. A pall of gloom covered Summer Ho and nothing we would do would lighten it.

I grew heavy with child and Harry and I grew further apart with my expanding waist. In January we heard that Hopton had had a victory at Braddock Down, and Harry and Ashley were eager to be off and back to the excitement of war, but the roads were still impassable with the winter's mud and they were forced to cool their impatient heels by wandering local lanes.

They were absent much from home and indeed I seemed only to see Harry during the long, dark evenings and, even then, he took to staying out later and later, forcing me to the conclusion that there was little in common between us. I heard from Meg that they spent

44

much of their time at the inn in the village which, as it was placed at the crossroads from Alton and Winchester, caught whatever traffic there might be.

Knowing I was ungainly with approaching motherhood and that my mind had grown dull and heavy with my body, I could understand that Harry sought for livelier company and yet my pillow was often wet with tears as I lay abed listening for the sound of returning horses.

Matters came to a head one day when I found both men in the great hall obviously preparing to go out and, losing my temper, I managed things badly.

'I wish you to stay in today,' I said more imperiously than I had intended. 'I would have your company, Harry.'

'How so, sweetheart? You have the Dame and Letty—and womanly matters to occupy you.'

'I have wish for my husband,' I repeated doggedly.

'Didst hear, Ashley? You are not one of this command.'

'How could I be, not being a lady's spouse?'

'Harry—'

'Another day, my love. I have business to attend to. The home farm needs a visit.'

'Please, Harry,' my voice trembled and I let a tear escape and slide down my cheek, which is what I should have done in the first place. I laid a hand on his arm and looked up entreatingly.

'Best count yourself routed,' advised a lazy voice from behind us. 'The lady asks prettily and you know that one in an interesting condition should never be frustrated, be her desire never so strange.'

' 'Tis no strange thing that I wish to have my husband to stay with me,' I flashed, anger sharpening my tone.

Over my head the men exchanged a glance and at once Harry slipped an arm about me and drew me towards the parlour.

'A game of Chance will please you? I think the cards were left in here.'

The morning passed pleasantly while I basked in the unaccustomed pleasure of my husband's company. We lunched together and then I lay down for my usual rest, but when I came downstairs again, Harry was nowhere to be found.

Ashley proffered no knowledge of his whereabouts and so it was that when my pains took me suddenly and agonisingly, Ashley it was that carried me to my bedchamber and summoned Meg to me.

All through the succeeding hours when I struggled to bear my child, in the moments I had to spare from pain and exhaustion, it was not Harry's face that was in my mind, but Ashley Death's long black eyes as he carried me in his arms up the stairs to my room.

In those days women were left to bear their children how they would. In big towns such as

London, there might be a few who practised midwifery but, in the country, one made do with female friends and servants or perhaps a local crone or 'white witch' who was versed in childbirth. Mourning bedclothes and black scarves were put ready with the cradle and baby clothes. However I was lucky and, early next morning, my daughter was born. Pink and mewing, she was put into my arms and I knew a wave of such satisfaction and love as I had never imagined before.

'What shall we call her?' I asked Harry when he visited me.

'Mary is a good loyal name,' he answered and so my little Mally was named, for so all Mary's were nicknamed.

'Are you pleased?' I asked hopefully, gazing fondly at the minute babe sleeping in the crook of my arm.

'Of course.'

I lifted my eyes sharply at the perfunctory note in his voice, to study the face of the man beside the bed. His hair was as golden as ever but his countenance seemed a shade more florid than of old and there was no doubting the sullen droop to his lip, reminding me of a child disappointed in his Christmas treat.

'I would better have had a boy,' he said at last. 'A man needs an heir at such a time as this.'

'You should give thanks for your wife's safe delivery,' said Dame Allis from her seat beside

47

the fire. She spoke severely and he had the grace to flush a little.

'I do—and pray that she bears a boy next time.'

'That was hardly tactful,' I remarked to Dame Allis after he had gone, 'to talk of the next time, and my body still sore and tired from this babe.'

'He was disappointed!' she defended him. 'Some men can accept daughters, but others need a son to prove their manhood. He'll come round, you'll see, and be as besotted by his pretty babe as any doting father.'

But as it happened, a summons came from Prince Rupert within a few days. He was in the west country and had need of every man in his attack on the Parliament forces. Harry and Ashley with their men made ready and unable, or uncaring, to hide their jubilation at the prospect of more excitement, rode off and Summer Ho returned to a quiet haven of womenfolk. I nursed my babe and wrapped myself in a cocoon of maternal domesticity unaware how soon the war was to come to our quiet part of Hampshire.

CHAPTER FIVE

After the men had left, Lettice seemed unduly silent but, putting it down to disappointment that Denzil had not managed to visit her more often during the relatively peaceful winter months, I was not particularly worried. But when several days had gone by and she still moped about the house, refusing either to eat or go out, I decided that something must be done. Dame Allis and I put our heads together and, knowing that Letty had neither the patience or inclination for work that would take long, contrived to find the materials for a set of stumpwork pictures to cover a box. I drew outlines on the linen and managed to make them bear some resemblance to Letty herself and Denzil standing amid a wild and romantic garden.

Lettice proclaimed herself pleased with our efforts and spent a happy morning with the silks and beads upon her lap planning where they should go before beginning upon the work itself with more energy and interest than I'd seen her display for some time.

I was making new gowns for Mally, who delighted my heart by growing apace, and we worked together in silence for a while, only the homely sound of scissors snipping thread or the thin hum as silk was pulled through cloth, breaking across our thoughts.

'Are you happy, Anne?'

I was startled by her abrupt question and answered truthfully before I had given it consideration, 'Sometimes.'

'I meant in your marriage?'

'I have a sweet baby—Summer Ho is all that I could wish for, and Dame Allis is very dear to me.'

'And Harry? What of him?'

'Harry is—Harry,' I spread my hands helplessly. 'I doubt that I can make him more homeloving, at least while this wretched war continues, so needs must constrain myself to accept him as he is and be thankful that he is fond of me!'

'But do you *love* him?' In her interest she dropped her work to the floor and leaned forward.

'Of course!' I made answer and bent over my needlework, unable to meet her eyes. 'But why all these questions?'

Instead of answering me she sprang to her feet, ignoring silks and materials which she scattered over the floor, and moved restlessly to the window. 'Don't you ever wish for something to happen?' she asked over her shoulder. 'I vow that if General Waller himself rode under the gatehouse, I'd be pleased to see him.'

'There are rumours that he is much abroad in Hampshire looking for any Cavaliers that would resist him, and seeking provender and money from all.'

'If only Denzil would take me to Oxford...'

''Tis only because he thinks of your welfare that he would have you stay here.'

'Nonsense, he is enjoying himself. Ashley

50

was telling me some tales he'd heard about Oxford. Not the King's Court of course, he thinks of nothing but that pious wife of his, but the society that is forced to live in the inns there.'

'I'm sure you do Denzil a wrong.'

She looked at me and shrugged. 'Perhaps you are right. I'd almost think more of him if he did amuse himself in such a way. Denzil is dull and staid and expects me to be the same.' Letty blew on a pane of glass and drew on it with one finger. 'Before all this trouble began we spent some time at our London house and even at home I had my friends and we gave dinners and had people to stay—our house was never empty.'

'I'm sorry you are bored!' I said stiffly, 'but with the times as they are and friends afraid to move from their own fireside, I scarcely feel I can entertain.'

She looked at me, lifting her eyebrows. 'What a little spitfire you have become, Anne. When I first arrived you were as quiet as a mouse, though I suspected you were not as meek as you seemed.'

'I'm sorry if you think I spoke unkindly,' I said calmly, knowing she was right. A few months ago I would not have spoken so. Then I had been ready to please and be pleased by all, but now I had grown up and was more settled in my position at Summer Ho. And while at first Letty had fascinated me with her fashionable clothes and stylish ways, over the months I had found how shallow she was and her endless complaining and pettish laments had begun to irritate me. Only occasionally in the last weeks had she bothered to show her charm and that had not been for my benefit.

'If only something would happen,' she said, and, seeing that she had lost interest in our slight quarrel, I turned back to my sewing.

As it happened, Summer Ho was to have excitement soon and in a way that held little pleasure for me. The day it happened I had been out riding and was just returning home, when I met a cow hurrying along the lane in a very unbovine manner. When I drew nearer I could see that her haste was caused by the attentions of a small boy who hurried her from the rear.

'How now?' I asked, blocking the way until my curiosity was answered.

'Soldiers, lady,' he answered, dancing impatiently from one bare foot to another. 'Soldiers be come to the village.'

'What kind? Ours or those of the Parliament?'

By his blank expression I saw that all soldiers were alike to him and probably as much trouble in his small world. 'Me Mam has sent me into the woods with our Daisy until they be gone. I'm to stay until she do send me word.'

'On your way, then,' I said moving Mab out

of his path, and then thought of something, 'What coats did the soldiers wear?'

'Red, m'lady.'

Almost before his answer had left his lips, I had set my heels into Mab's sides and was forcing her into a gallop towards home. Once under the gatehouse, it was the work of moments to call for the grooms and to shout a warning to the steward. Soon all the horses and the house cow were being driven out of their stables and through the gate into the home park. The Roundheads, I hoped, would not have time to search for them, even if they suspected their presence. When the animals had left and the sounds of their hoofs and the hastening shouts from the groom and stable boy had begun to die away, I picked up my heavy skirt and ran into the house. Here I found the servants were already transporting the best of our provisions up to the attics, where they could be hidden in a dusty corner, and Dame Allis intent upon collecting silver plate.

'What will you do with it?' I asked, gathering up an armful of mugs and dishes and then, realising that two arms could never carry so much, scooped up the hem of my skirt and bundled the silver into the bag thus formed.

'I have a place,' she answered cryptically, and sailed from the hall her arms full.

With my burden knocking against my knees, I clanked after her and followed to her bedchamber where I found her on her knees in the middle of the floor.

'Bolt the door,' she commanded, looking up briefly.

And when I turned back from having obeyed her, I saw a widening gap at her feet as she lifted up one of the broad planks that formed the floor.

'My husband used to keep his money here,' she said, busily laying the plate in the black hole, 'but all the servants of his time have long since died. I'll lay wager that I am the only one to remember this hiding place.'

She crammed in a last candlestick and together we put back the floorboard and trundled her chair to cover it before she took her seat, only the high spots of colour on her cheeks and quickened breathing to betray the activity of the last few minutes.

'And here I stay until they go,' she said, spreading her wide skirts and settling her wig aright. ''Twould take General Waller himself to move me.'

I ran to the window and peered out over the gatehouse towards the road.

'Are they here yet? No—well you'd best change into a gown. Your riding habit would be hard to explain with no horses in the stables.'

What perversity made me choose my richest, most becoming gown, I'll never know. Perhaps I wished to show, with my silks and laces, that I

54

was not afraid—-or perhaps, womanlike, I merely wanted to look and feel my best to give me confidence for the coming ordeal. Whatever it was, I flung off my riding habit and, hurling it in a corner as I called for Meg, pushed open a chest and began hunting through the contents.

As I pulled cool, soft pink folds over my head, the sound of hooves clattering over the cobbled yard came to our ears and, for a moment, I was still as my eyes met Meg's. Then I settled the skirt, thrust my arms into the sleeves and turned to be laced into the bodice. As I pinned on my lace collar, Tom Holwell tapped at the door. 'A Captain Everton is below and would have word with you.'

'I will be down anon,' I answered and was pleased at the calm of my voice, though my hands trembled as I twisted my back hair into a bun and teased the side pieces into loose tendrils. My eyes stared back at me from the looking glass, dark and wide with apprehension. 'Now a dab of scent,' I said, stretching my wrists to Meg 'and I am ready.'

As I descended the stairs, the man in the hall turned and swept the black broadbrimmed hat from his head. He stood looking up at me and, as I slowly approached, I had time to examine his appearance. Not so tall as Harry, he was slim and straight, his shoulders broad under the red tunic. As he stepped forward and bowed, his hair gleamed red in a stray shaft of sunlight.

'Captain Everton, mistress. At your service.'

'You wished to see me?' I asked coldly, pausing on the last step, very conscious of the picture I made in my pale gown against the dark brown of the old panelling.

'The steward told me that the master of the house is not available.'

'He is away from home,' I said blandly, meeting a glance from shrewd grey eyes.

'Indeed? 'Tis to be hoped that these troubled times do not disturb his journey.'

'I am sure they won't, but surely you didn't come to discuss his travels.'

'I come for provender. My troop has need of supplies.'

'You'll find very little here.'

'Oh, come, madam—a house this size and fully stocked.'

''Tis the end of spring—our winter stocks are used up and this is the hard time of year.'

'We'll be content with what you have— bread and cheese will do for the men, and the horses can crop grass in your park.'

His grey eyes were watching me intently and I knew that I could not attempt to refuse. To antagonise him would be foolish and I had the feeling that he would be an implacable enemy.

'Tell your men to come to the kitchen and I'll make arrangements for them to be fed there—do you intend to stay long?'

'Till morning.'

His curt answer made no attempt at the pretence of asking my permission and, for the first time, I began to realise that Summer Ho was occupied by members of the opposing army.

'Doubtless then you'll wish for a chamber to be prepared for you,' I said, hoping in this way to persuade him that I had nothing to hide. 'We dine at five—will you join us?'

He bent his red head slightly. 'My pleasure—but first I must ask you for your keys.'

'My keys?' I asked blankly, 'but why? I will give you all that is necessary.'

'Doubtless—but you must realise that we are on different sides and, as such, I must search this house.'

'We have nothing to hide, I do assure you. I'd hardly keep a troop of Royalists in the attics,' I said hotly, and then could have bitten out my tongue for having mentioned the hiding place of so much that was valuable.

Captain Everton strode towards me, his heavy boots creaking as he moved. 'Your keys, ma'am,' he said implacably, one hand outstretched.

I hesitated, glancing fleetingly up at his face and then dropping my own eyes beneath his hard grey gaze, reluctantly placed my keys in his waiting palm.

'I'll return them before we leave,' he said, and bowing curtly he left the Great Hall to issue orders to his men.

For the next few hours havoc reigned in Summer Ho. Dame Allis shut herself in her chamber, with good reason as I well knew, and so did Lettice with less cause. I arranged for a meal to be provided for the troopers and a room made ready for their Captain. Everywhere one met with Rebel soldiers. They were to be seen emerging dusty and covered in grime from the cellars or attics, every chamber was thoroughly searched but luckily only a cheese and a few jars of preserves were their reward.

At my insistence, Lettice presented herself at the dinner table and Dame Allis, having agreed that to remain in the Queen's Chamber would arouse suspicion, seated herself beside the Roundhead officer. Letty remained silent throughout the meal but the older woman maintained a flow of conversation and all went well until the boards had been cleared and we prepared to leave our unwelcome guest to his wine. As I passed him, on the way to join Dame Allis and Letty, he put out a detaining hand.

'A word with you, mistress.' He strode across the room and closed the door onto the departing women, who had not realised that I had not accompanied them. 'I would prefer it to be in private, if you please.'

'It is hardly proper...' I began but was silenced as his voice cut above mine.

'Send for your duenna by all means, if you

must, but I would hardly have thought that now was the time for strict etiquette.'

I shrugged. 'What have you to say?'

'Won't you sit down?' He gestured to a chair beside the fire and I saw, for the first time, the lines of fatigue round his eyes. His shoulders drooped wearily and yet, while I stood, so must he.

'I prefer to stand,' I said and knew a small triumph as he sighed almost imperceptibly. 'Your business can only take a few minutes, surely?'

'As you will.' Putting his hands flat on the table, he leaned on his arms and looked at me over the lighted candles.

'Do you expect me to believe that you dine *en famille* off pewter plates? And ones so dull that this must be the first time they've seen the light of day for many a year.' Without waiting for a reply, he went on: 'And your larder so poorly stocked that we find you at starvation point?'

'I fear we are somewhat impoverished.'

'Impoverished! Are you so poor that you keep neither home cow or horses? The only creatures in your yard are a few scrawny chickens.'

'My husband is hoping to replenish our fortunes—that is why he is from home and, as for the cow, I'm afraid she took sick a few weeks ago and died.'

He stared at me, his eyes narrowing. 'And

59

yet you sport so rich a gown?' he asked slowly.

Glancing down at the pure silk, I bit my lip. ' 'Twas bought before our troubles...' I began, but my questioner straightened impatiently.

'I'll not detain you longer—doubtless I'll see you before I leave.'

The vague threat in his voice stayed with me all night, and next morning, when I awoke to a low bovine mooing from the courtyard, I knew his promise would be put into effect. I would have stayed in my room but, knowing he would send for me, and rather than obey his command, I went in search of him.

'Your dead cow has returned,' he said calmly when I found him on the steps above the courtyard supervising the mounting of his men. 'And two horses who appear to feel at home in your stables.'

Swiftly I turned and saw a soldier holding a horse we used to pull a cart and, beside him, Mab danced impatiently, eager to return to her warm stall and breakfast.

I looked back at Captain Everton and found him watching me closely. 'You'll not take the little grey?' I cried, making no pretence to disclaim the animals. 'She's too small for a man and not strong enough for use as a pack horse.'

'She's the right size for a drummer boy.'

I swallowed and closed my eyes while visions of my gay little horse among the horrors of warfare crossed my lids. Opening my eyes again, I realised that the soldier was still talking '... of course if we find a little more provender—say two cheeses—I might decide another horse was not so necessary.'

Looking down at me, he met my eyes blandly and, for the first time, I thought I saw amusement in his grey gaze. 'Two cheeses and a barrel of ale shall we say?'

And so the Roundheads rode under my gatehouse carrying some of our cherished provisions with them but Mab lay safe in the stable, while Dame Allis stretched her cramped limbs and rose from her chair over the hidden silver plate.

Hardly had they left and the house was put to rights, though we left the silver in its hiding place, than Harry and Ashley Death came riding into the courtyard. This time we women had our own adventure to recount, and much we made of it.

Harry vowed it was a privilege to go short of cheeses to hear such a story, and Letty never tired of telling how stricken she felt at the Roundheads' approach and how prostrate her nerves had been ever since. To my surprise, Ashley appeared to listen sympathetically, but I was too involved with my husband to spare them much of my interest, though I was to wish that I had done so later.

Harry seemed to have recovered from his disappointment at having a daughter and, as Mally was now an enchanting four months old, deigned to chuck her under her diminutive chin a few times and even allowed her to chew his finger now and then.

The war appeared to be going well for the Royalist side. General Hopton had had several victories, while Harry and Ashley, under Prince Rupert's command, had beaten the Roundheads at Chalgrovefield and so, being well in reach of Summer Ho, had travelled home for a well-earned rest from the war. They were only with us a few days, not long enough for any discord to arise and, as I waved from the front steps, I felt that they had been the happiest days of my marriage.

All too soon came news of more battles. Gloucester and Exeter were Royalist victories. Letty had received a letter at the same time and I noticed how strangely she behaved. Carrying it away to her chamber to read in private, not sharing her news as we all usually did, she was very silent at dinner that night and, after retiring at our usual early hour, I was disturbed by sounds of movement from her room. Thinking she was ill or worried by bad news, I put down the book I was reading and went to her.

As I opened her door, confusion met me. Dresses, shifts and petticoats were strewn about the room; ribbons, laces and shoes were scattered over the floor, while every drawer and chest was opened and spilling its contents. In the middle of the room, Letty knelt beside an open trunk, feverishly packing clothes into its already disordered interior.

'What's to do?' I cried. 'Is Denzil wounded? Why ever didn't you tell us?'

She threw me a haunted glance over her shoulder and turned back to her task without a word.

Closing the door behind me, I knelt beside her, taking a crumpled shift from her hands and folded it neatly. 'You'd best let me help,' I said, trying to make order of her untidy attempt.

Still without speaking, she left me and, going to the table, ran a comb through her disordered curls, then wet a finger and smoothed her fair eyebrows. Casting her a glance, I decided that she hardly had the appearance of one who had received bad news. On the contrary, there was an air of suppressed excitement, of brittle anticipation that intrigued me. I waited for her to speak and at last she said, 'You may as well know, I'm going away.'

'Indeed? 'Tis a little sudden, surely. I'd no idea that you were unhappy here but of course I can understand that you wish to be with your husband.'

She gave a short laugh and picked up a mirror. Not meeting my eyes, she adjusted a stray lock of hair and said into the mirror, 'There you have it wrong, sister—I go to Ashley.'

'Ashley!'

''Tis his letter I received. We have it all

63

arranged; a coach is waiting in the village and will come for me in the morning. I did but wait for him to find lodging.'

'But—you *can't*—what of Denzil?' I cried aghast at her duplicity.

Ignoring me, she picked up her jewel box and dropped it into the trunk while I tried to take in this information, uneasily aware that something akin to dismay filled me.

'Denzil?' She spoke the name as though never having heard it before. 'Denzil—oh, he will go on as before, my leaving him will make little difference to his mode of life. For long now I have been unnecessary to his welfare.'

'You do him wrong—'

'Little you know,' she broke in scornfully, 'so wrapped up in your husband and babe are you. What do you know of life—or loneliness?'

Perforce I had to agree with her and was silent until I said tentatively: 'You could have married Ashley once.'

'Fore God, how I wish I had!' she exclaimed and, hearing the emotion in her voice that usually held nothing more than pettish vapours, I felt a sympathy rise in me. 'There is nothing to be said,' she went on looking at me. 'I have made up my mind—Dame Allis—'

'Had best know nothing of this until after you have gone. 'Twill be better so.'

Letty agreed and so it was that I lay abed the next morning listening to the furtive movements in the room next door. Faintly the rumble of coach wheels carried to my ears and then silence returned to Summer Ho as Lettice left the house behind and set off on her adventure.

CHAPTER SIX

On 20th September, Essex and His Majesty's forces met at Newbury. The conflict was long and bitter and still undecided by nightfall. However, when the King withdrew, everyone concluded that the Parliamentary army had won. Of course we at Summer Ho heard nothing of this until much later when Harry arrived unexpectedly one morning. When he left a few days later, the rumours abounding held more hope for the Royalist side. Prince Rupert's brother, Maurice, had taken Dartmouth. Waller had failed to take the besieged Basing House, and Hopton was driving through the counties of Dorset, Hampshire and Wiltshire to clear them of Rebel troops.

Therefore, I was more than a little surprised when I came out of the stables after a ride on Mab to find Roundhead outriders just cantering into the courtyard.

'What do you?' I asked angrily, as the rest of the troop arrived, and I was surrounded by horses and riders.

The early December dusk was falling, the air heavy and chill. The animals snorted steam from their nostrils, and the men's faces were pinched with cold. The clunk of accoutrements and creak of leather filled the air. The troopers were too busy to take notice of me as I stood by, frustrated in my attempts to refuse them entry, and in danger of being trampled under the heavy hoofs of the animals.

'Take my stirrup,' commanded a voice above my head, and I was glad to obey, not looking up until I was safe on the steps by the door.

When I did look up, I saw the straight back of Captain Everton riding back into the mêlée and was momentarily disconcerted. I had felt sure of having seen the last of him, last May.

I lingered on the steps and, after a few moments, the apparently disorderly crowd dissolved into two neat lines of horses and men and, at a word, the riders dismounted and led their mounts into the stables. Seeing their officer heading towards the door of Summer Ho, I stayed where I was, firmly in the doorway, barring him entry.

He stopped a few steps from the top and looked gravely at me. My heart missed a beat as I realised why I had not recognised him at first. He was wearing the iron pot helmet that I'd heard so much about, and that was such a distinguishing feature of the Parliament forces. Behind the metal faceguard his eyes were alert and watchful.

'Give you good morrow, Mistress Summer,' he said slowly.

'What would you, now, Captain Everton?' I asked sharply. 'You make free of my stables; do you intend to use my house also?'

'We do wish for lodging, yes.' He looked at me warily and obviously made an effort to be conciliatory. 'Let us deal amicably together,' he suggested, pulling off his great gauntleted gloves and tucking them into his belt.

'Needs must—but I warn you, sir, I feel hardly amicable,' I warned.

'No time to hide the plate?' he asked and flashed me a glance before turning away to issue orders to his men.

My keys were again demanded and somehow we all fitted into some kind of routine. Dame Allis and I saw little of Captain Everton, save in the evenings when he dined with us. The soldiers seemed to spend the days in scouring the countryside, returning as dusk fell, tired and mudsplattered, laden with weapons and driving acquired horses. From this, Dame Allis and I deduced that some new battle was imminent and would be fought nearby. Our prayer was that Harry would not choose now to ride home and find his house occupied by his enemies. I wrote in haste to him and sent the little stable boy off to the last address I had. I took to spending much of my own day in the saddle, though I was pregnant again and should not have done so, and rode far afield anxiously scouring the roads around Summer Ho for gaily clad riders. After leaving messages at various outlying farms that were friendly, there was not much else I could do and, curbing my worry, I *waited*.

Matters came to a head one night after we had retired. Captain Everton had not appeared at dinner, being closeted in the stables with his men, as Tom Holwell my steward reported. Dame Allis and I spent a worried evening playing pique in a desultory fashion and had then gone to bed but, in my case at least, not to sleep. Pulling a furlined cloak about me, I blew out the candle and, seating myself on the windowseat, peered out at the black night from behind the curtains.

I had not long to wait. Quite soon the stable doors opened and horses and men appeared. Within minutes, and with little sound, they had mounted and ridden under the gatehouse to vanish into the frosty night.

'They've ridden away!' I cried, bursting into Dame Allis' bedchamber. 'Where do you think they've gone?'

She hadn't been asleep and sat up quickly at my entry.

'It must be a town—we have no big houses near, unless it be Basing House they aim for.' She pursed her lips. 'More like Alton or Winchester methinks—but to travel at night! 'Tis unheard of!'

'Not so—General Waller has been nicknamed "the Night Owl" for his liking for night marches and he lies within reach at Farnham.' Going to the window I pulled aside the thick curtains and looked out at the silent night. My breath misted the diamond shaped pane, but not before I'd seen the bright overhead stars and twinkling frosty ground. 'Think you they will be back?'

'Who knows?' she shrugged, hitching the bedclothes high. 'You'd best away to your bed, my girl, or you'll catch a chill. In your condition this anxiety will lose you the babe.'

Taking her advice, I hurried back to my room and curled up in the warm centre of my bed. The brick was still hot and I snuggled my icy toes on it, waiting for sleep to come.

I awoke, heavy and dull, with a raging headache; Dame Allis was as worried as I and, after a few remarks, we avoided each other's company by mutual consent. It was not until the second day after they had ridden away that we had any news, and then rumours filled the village of a battle at Alton, but it was not until the soldiers returned that it was confirmed.

They rode wearily into the courtyard, drooping in the saddles, the horses dark with sweat. Captain Everton saw the men and horses settled and then came slowly up the steps and into the hall.

The candles in their sconces flared in the draught as he opened the door and, in the sudden brightness, I saw a bandage was tied round one hand. He dragged off his helmet and dropped it on the table, running a hand through his red hair as he turned to the fire. Seeing me in the shadows, he stopped abruptly and made an attempt to straighten his tired shoulders.

'You are hurt,' I said coming forward.

He looked at his hand as if he had never seen it before.

''Tis nothing, a mere scratch.'

'Best sit down while I get water and linen,' I commanded, and whisked out of the room on my self-imposed errand.

He had spoken truly, the wound was very little more than a scratch, but long and deep across the palm of his left hand.

'You've been into battle?' I asked needlessly as I bathed his hand. The Parliamentarian nodded and drank the wine I'd placed at his elbow. 'Can I ask where?'

'Alton,' he answered baldly, and into the silence I said, 'Will you tell me more?'

At first he did not answer and I thought that I was to hear no more. Nothing was said while I bandaged his hand and the silence lasted until I'd set down the scissors and begun to clear away the bowl of bloodied water then, as I arose, he put out a detaining hand.

'You may as well know—we had the victory.' Clasping my hands in front of me on the table, I sat down as he went on. 'We took

70

the Royalists by surprise. They expected the attack from the direction of Farnham and during the day. We attacked from Chawton and early in the first light. The battle lasted for hours—midday at least, and by then we'd fought our way up the main street towards the Church, trapping Colonel Bolles and his men there...' He made a strangely helpless gesture. 'He and most of his men were killed.'

'In the Church!' I cried, shocked.

'War has no time for niceties.'

''Tis no nicety but pure decency!' I burst out. 'To fight in a Church is unheard of.'

'Spare me your histrionics,' he spoke wearily. ''Tis time you realised that war is neither honourable or fair—it is unscrupulous and dishonest, dirty and bloody.' He stopped and pulled himself to his feet, leaning both hands on the table before pushing himself upright and heading for the door. 'I shall see to my men and be grateful for a meal when I return,' he said over his shoulder.

Strangely enough, although he had been fighting, and perhaps killing, Cavaliers, I felt more kindly disposed towards Captain Everton than I had before. His wound and obvious dislike for warfare made me see him as a man rather than just an enemy, someone to be cheated and disliked merely because he was a Roundhead.

Mally, at nine months old, was surviving the dangers of teething, and growing more like

71

her father every day. I found that I liked motherhood and looked forward to the time when a brother or sister would join her in the nursery. The anxiety and exercise of the last few days seemed to have had no untoward effect and, God willing, my second babe would be born at the end of June. While realising that Harry's absences at war were likely to limit our children and remembering the dangers of infancy and childhood, I hoped for a full nursery to make sure of being survived by a few children at least. To lose an only child must be agony but the loss of one of several could doubtless be borne more easily.

Dame Allis seemed to find great delight in her great granddaughter, playing with her by the hour. She scarcely mentioned Letty. We heard from Harry that she and Ashley were living together, she following him about the countryside and lodging where she could. Of Denzil we heard nothing and knew not how he viewed the departure of his wife, but supposed the loss would not affect him deeply.

What I thought in the matter I hardly knew myself. I'll not deny that I found the thought of Ashley and Letty together none to my liking. Ashley was a man of the world and undoubtedly intelligent, while Letty, having an air of fashion, was not gifted with either brains or deep emotions. I could have hoped that Ashley Death had found another mate and with her more chance of happiness.

The Parliamentarians stayed with us for several days, nursing their wounds, refurbishing their weapons and repairing the horses' shoes and tackle. I saw little of Captain Everton until the last day when he came to me and offered a bill for the provender they had used.

'Will it be honoured?' I asked drily, fingering the sheet of closely written paper.

'You'll have to send to London—but to be honest, I believe that payment is difficult to come by,' he answered. 'I would advise you to keep hold of the paper and not let it out of your sight.'

Carefully folding the paper, I nodded and, going to one of the blue-white ginger jars that stood over the fireplace, dropped it inside. 'I'll keep it safe and hope it will be redeemed one day!'

He settled his helmet over his red hair and, picking up his heavy leather gloves, made a move to go. 'I hope we haven't proved too much of a nuisance?'

Making a polite disclaimer, I wondered why he waited. Still hesitating, he toyed with his gloves and then said 'Perhaps, some day, we may meet under better circumstances?'

I lifted my eyebrows. 'I hardly see how that can happen, sir,' I said slowly.

'After this war is over...'

'My husband will return home and we shall take up our usual lives,' I put in before he could finish. I spoke hastily, having no wish for his tentative offer of friendship—or something more.

He withdrew at once and, touching a hand to his helmet in ironical salute, bid me 'goodbye' and strode from the room, leaving me wondering just what he had been about to say. Going to the window, I watched from behind the curtains as the Roundheads mounted and rode away. As his horse trotted under the gatehouse, he half turned and looked up at my window. A premonition seized me that I had not seen the last of Captain Everton but how important a role he was to play in my life I had no idea.

I had little time to wonder about him or anything else for, within a few days, Dame Allis took to her bed and, seeing her thin grey face against the pillows, I could not deceive myself that she was anything but seriously ill. Sending for the nearest apothecary in Alton, I realised that I was making a fruitless gesture and that, even if he arrived in time, there was little he could do to still the effects of a long life.

'You're wasting your time, my girl,' she said when I told her. 'No-one can cure old age.'

'You'll feel better tomorrow,' I soothed, taking one of her restless hands in mine.

She shook her head against the pillows, and I thought how strange she looked with her head in a nightcap rather than the familiar red wig.

'No matter,' she said. 'I've had my life—and

74

enjoyed it. My only regret is that I must leave it without knowing that Harry is safe.' Turning her head, she looked at me with bright intelligent eyes. 'You're a wench after my own heart, Anne—and a good wife to my grandson.'

'I try to be.'

'I know things are sometimes difficult—men were ever so. One man satisfies us, but men have a greater need that we can satisfy. Remember that and don't blame him too much.'

I opened my mouth to ask her what she meant, but she hurried on almost as if she didn't want me to question her. She pulled at my hand to regain my attention and now her voice was growing tired.

'Leave the plate where it is, 'tis safe enough there. There's another hiding place. I've kept it to myself, but now 'tis best that you should know in case you have need of it. 'Twas made in the old Queen's reign, before she gave the house to us. It's hid none save a Papist priest— but now—it might be of use again.'

Her voice died away and I waited for a few minutes for her to go on before asking 'Where is it?'

'The Great Hall. On either side of the fireplace is carved a bunch of grapes. Twist the right one to release the catch and then the back of the fireplace can be opened like a door. 'Tis a passage, not a room, and leads under the house

75

and out into the home wood…'

She stopped, and her heavy breathing told me that she was asleep. Gently I released her hand and tidied the coverlet higher around her thin shoulders, realising how old she had grown in the last few weeks.

Next evening, having nothing better to do and no-one around, I set about finding the secret passage. The bunch of grapes proved easy to manipulate but, although the door behind the fire moved a trifle, it failed to open as I had imagined it would. Catching up my skirts, I stepped over the ashes of the fire and put my hand to the warm stone. Still it resisted my efforts and at last I slipped my fingers into the dark oracle and slowly pushed it open. Lifting my candle high, I peered into the dark hold. A rush of cold air made the flame flicker as it was blown out, but not before I had seen a narrow tunnel that led down into thick velvet blackness. Grey cobwebs waved in the draught and a huge spider scuttled away as I drew back, wondering how to close the opening.

Closer inspection showed me a small indentation just big enough for the tips of my fingers. Pulling on this, the door slid back into place and once again the secret door was indiscernible from the other blocks of stone that formed the back of the fireplace, and I was filled with admiration for the man who had made the Priests' hole.

Early in the New Year, Dame Allis died. We

had received letters from Harry the day before and she had fallen asleep still clasping hers. Looking at the narrow figure in the bed with thin hands crossed and sharp nose jutting towards the ceiling, I knew I had lost a friend and wept bitterly. Now I was alone in Summer Ho. With my dear Dame dead and Letty away following her lover, I had no other gentlewoman to sustain me, and precious few servants, save my invaluable Meg and Tom Holwell. But even this was not the end of my sorrows.

Dame Allis had been carried to the family tomb, and I was sitting, trying to write to Harry, when Tom entered and said there was a person to see me.

'I think 'tis the wench from the home farm,' he said at my inquiring look.

'Betty Green? What can she want? No matter, send her in,' and laying aside my writing materials, I looked to the door, glad for anything that might relieve my gloom.

The girl entered quickly, without the sullenness I remembered. She was carrying a bundle under her cloak and I knew a moment's surprise when it mewed and I realised it was a baby.

She bobbed an awkward curtsey and then stood joggling the babe in her arms.

'What do you want, Betty?' I asked kindly, already reaching for my purse. 'A guinea for your mother's baby?'

Pale blue eyes looked at me and she licked her lips. ' 'Tis mine, not me mam's,' she said.

'Oh well—such things happen,' I murmured, willing to be broad-minded and mindful of the soldiers that had stayed with us. Did the dates fit, I wondered vaguely, and then realised that the girl was talking.

'Granfer has died and Da is going to take his farm, so we're leaving the home farm.'

'I see, but surely your father should have come and told me himself. We need time to find a new tenant. Times are difficult and good farmers hard to find.'

'They sent me,' she answered, and now I could see the sullen droop returning to her lip. 'Really?' I said, lifting my brows. 'The master will not be pleased.'

'You must take the baby,' she suddenly burst out, and abruptly placed the tiny child on the table between us.

I stared at her. 'Are you mad?'

'I've called 'im Harry,' she said and, lifting her head, stared defiantly at me.

Slowly her meaning dawned on me and I dragged my gaze away from hers to stare at the baby. Reluctantly I reached over the polished wood and pushed aside the coverings. A tiny wizened face came into view and as I looked, two bright familiar blue eyes. I had no need to look at the soft golden down that covered his head. Quite suddenly I knew beyond all doubt who was his father.

'You'll keep him.' It was a statement rather than a question, and, as I lifted my eyes, she said quietly, ''Tis that—or the pond. I've no use for him.' Looking down at him, she went on dispassionately, 'Did my best to get rid of 'im I did but he were determined to be born, so I thought as I'd give him a chance.'

She crossed to the door and said over her shoulder, 'He'll be company for your girl'—Her knowing eyes passed over me—'and the new babe.'

She was gone before I could reply—even if I had anything to say. My world was falling in ruins; already I had found the date of the child's conception, *June*, when Harry and I had been so happy together and I thought, in my innocence, that we had found a lasting love.

CHAPTER SEVEN

And so little Hal, for I could not bring myself to call him Harry, came to live at Summer Ho. I managed to find him a wet nurse from the village but she was reluctant either to live in or to travel each day and, against my better judgement, I weaned him as soon as I could. He seemed to thrive on diluted cow's milk sucked through a scrap of linen from a cow's horn and, to my surprise, was a happy, contented child. Mally accepted him at once, with no signs of jealousy at sharing her nursery; perhaps she was too young to realise that he might prove a rival.

I took up my pen many times to write to Harry but each time the letter I sent contained no mention of the baby. I could find no words to tell him, and his own letters were as loving and brief as ever.

Letty had been gone for more than half a year and I'd heard no news of her, but Ashley was to cross my path again and unexpected tragedy was to follow in his wake.

All of Hampshire was in General Waller's hands, this being the reason for Harry remaining away, and life in our part of the country was relatively peaceful until just after Mally's first birthday when the armies started marching again.

On the 29th March I was called to the window by the thunder of galloping horses and looked out in time to see a group of Cavaliers racing by in what could only be retreat. Setting out linen and salves, I waited to treat any wounded who might ask for aid, but none came and I concluded that the Roundhead pursuit was too close to permit any stopping save for the most desperate reason.

The early spring evening was just falling, when sounds of hooves brought me to the window. The animal's faltering pace told me that he was near done for, and even as I watched, his rider jumped from his back, tore his hat from his head and urged his frightened mount on past the house. Throwing a quick backwards glance over his shoulder, he ran across the road and, a moment later, emerged from the shadows gathering under the gatehouse.

With a premonition of disaster, I arose from the windowseat and, running downstairs, opened the front door. A slim figure slipped inside and leaned against the heavy oak while he recovered his breath.

'My apologies, Anne,' he panted. 'I should not have come, save that my business is the King's and 'tis imperative that I be not caught.'

'Ashley!' I gasped and then, with a rush of fear, 'Are you hurt—wounded?'

'Nay, neither, 'tis my horse that foundered at your gate.' Taking both my hands in his, he held them in a firm grasp and drew me to the window. For a moment he studied my face and then, despite his evident weariness, smiled. 'It's good to see you,' he said.

Against my will, I smiled back. I could feel a warmth filling my heart and an idiot's grin stretching my mouth. Afraid of the feelings that threatened to overwhelm me, I sought for a means to break the charged atmosphere around us and asked cruelly 'What of Letty? How does she?'

The grip on my hands tightened and the smile left his eyes. 'Well enough,' he answered evenly. His gaze travelled over me. 'I see you

81

are about to produce again—motherhood becomes you.'

I pulled my hands free and swung away. 'You make me sound like a prize cow!' I cried.

'Admit you asked for it and we'll cry pax! And, indeed, we have no time for quarrelling!' His voice deepened and he moved closer, looking down at me in the gathering gloom. 'I'd liefer we parted friends.'

Involuntarily I put out my hand. 'And I,' I whispered. 'And I.'

My fingers were carried to his lips and then retained in a warm clasp as he led me to the settle and, constraining me to sit, sat down beside me. 'We must to business. We've had a defeat at Cheriton. Can you get me away, Anne? Have you a horse?'

'Only Mab, or a farmhorse we use for a cart. I doubt me that Mab is up to your weight but the carthorse is slow and not used to the saddle. What think you?'

He pondered briefly. 'Mab it will have to be. I'm sorry to take your horse but I must make speed.'

'Go and saddle her. 'Tis best if no-one else knows you've been here—or left!' I said, standing up. 'Have you time for wine or food?'

'My thanks but neither—I must away. The Rebels are close on my tail.'

And, as though we were in a play and his words a cue, approaching horsebeats drummed the road. For a second his eyes held mine and then he jumped to his feet. 'They mustn't find me here,' he said, hurrying to the door. 'I'll try to get to the home park, and not implicate you.'

I stopped him as he lifted the latch. 'There's no time—they're almost at the gate.'

One brown hand fumbled at his sword and then, looking at me, his hand fell away from the hilt and I knew he would not resist because of me.

'There is a way,' I cried, both hands on his arm, urging him toward the fireplace. 'There's a Priests' hole behind the fire. Dame Allis said it led to the home park.' I pulled at the bunch of grapes and the door behind the fireplace opened.

Ashley looked hesitantly at the black opening. 'Are you sure ...?' he began doubtfully.

'No, I'm not,' I answered truthfully. 'The way might be blocked or dangerous, but 'tis that—or capture.' Thrusting a candlestick into his hand, I pushed him impatiently towards the passage.

His dark eyes glinted down into mine. The flickering candle flame highlighted his still vivid scar as he bent his head towards me. Gripping my head with one hand, he kissed me full on the mouth and then, stepping quickly over the fire, pushed wider the secret door and, without a backwards glance, vanished into its dark depths.

Gently touching my lips with the back of my fingers, I reached over the low fire and closed the gap in the stone. Scarcely had I time to step back than horses clattered into the courtyard and heavy fists crashed against the front door.

Excited voices demanded entry as I crossed the room and, with trembling hands, pulled back the bolts. The door was thrust open and immediately the Great Hall was filled with men in shining metal breastplates and pot helmets.

'Has anyone been here?' demanded a familiar voice, and I found myself looking up into the cold grey eyes of Captain Everton. Without waiting for my reply, he turned back to his men and ordered them to search the house.

'How dare you?' I cried above the tumult as heavy boots marched across the floorboards. 'What are you looking for?'

He looked at me briefly before moving restlessly about the room. 'A King's Messenger.'

'What makes you think he would be here? True, I have seen fleeing Cavaliers, but none have stopped.'

'Have I your word?'

Avoiding his eyes, I nodded. 'Yes, no-one has come here.'

A terse silence made me turn to look at the Parliamentarian and, as I did so, he bent to pick up something from the floor by the settle. With it in his hand he straightened and looked at me.

'You say no-one has been here?' he asked abruptly.

I hesitated and then said defiantly, 'Yes.'

'Then, madam, I must give you the lie!' His voice was harsh and he crossed the room quickly. Standing very close he thrust one hand towards me and reluctantly I lowered my eyes to look at what he held.

' 'Tis my husband's,' I whispered, unable to tear my eyes away from the glove so near to my face.

'As it's warm and still wet with sweat, I can only conclude that Master Summer is the man we seek.'

I closed my eyes against the implacable face above me. 'No, no, I swear he is with Prince Rupert.'

'Swear away, your word holds little truth for me.'

As I sank down on the settle, I heard him moving about the room which seemed to have grown suddenly dark. Abruptly, lights sprang up as Captain Everton pushed a taper into the fire and then lit the candles in their sconces. Involuntarily my eyes strayed to the fireplace and then I felt myself grow cold with horror. A black crack had appeared in the stones behind the fire. In my haste the secret door had obviously not closed properly.

While various men returned and reported no success, I sat and watched the betraying opening like a mesmerised hare, fearing he might follow my gaze, yet unable to tear away my eyes. Captain Everton moved about, looking behind tapestries, sounding the panelling with his knuckle and fingering the carving. I knew that it was only a matter of time until he found the secret door and wondered how far along its dark length was Ashley Death. Could he be near the end? Remembering how far away was the home wood, and realising that the way was unknown and perhaps treacherous, I knew that he could not have reached the end and safety.

Leaning back with an assumption of ease, and hoping he would not notice my hands that seemed to clasp and unclasp of their own accord, I asked with the air of a hostess at a great levee, 'Will you take wine?'

Briefly his eyes flickered towards me. 'No thank you.'

'Then I shall,' I said brightly and, walking across the room to the sideboard, poured wine into a glass. I noticed his eyes followed me and that he moved slightly so that I was clearly within his range of vision.

'To success!' I toasted ambiguously and, seeing his eyes narrow, knew that I had succeeded in gaining his attention. 'Yours now but ours *last*.'

'At the moment we are in the ascent, 'twould be as well for you to remember that.'

'What mean you?' I asked trying to still the

quaver in my voice.

'That you'd show more sense by helping us in our search.' Briefly his eyes fell to my spreading waist. 'No-one would blame a woman in your condition.'

'La, sir! What can you know of such things,' I exclaimed, and knew surprise at the echo of Letty that sounded in my voice.

'I left my wife awaiting the birth of our third child and, for her sake, would not treat you unkindly. However, I am determined not to leave here without our quarry, and will search this house 'til dawn if necessary. We will begin with this hall; believe me, ma'am, we shall find him however unpleasant for you.'

He turned away, calling for his men and I knew that within a few moments the secret door would be found unless I could do something. Wildly my mind sought for a way of distraction, anything to gain a few more moments.

'I have your permission to retire?' I asked, crossing to the stairs with a nicely calculated assumption of eagerness in my walk. 'If you have no need of me here, I will go to my chamber.'

Captain Everton looked thoughtfully at me and I deliberately allowed my gaze to falter and my breathing to quicken.

'Wait!' he commanded and came to where I paused with one hand on the newel post. 'Where would you suggest we started our search? he asked.

'Really, sir!' I laughed, 'do you expect me to tell you that?' For a moment I looked into his eyes which were near level with my own, and then glanced about the Great Hall. 'Here, I suppose, is as good a place as any,' and again I made to climb the stairs, but again he detained me, placing one brown hand over mine as I held the banisters. Perforce I paused, lifting my chin and asked disdainfully, 'What would you, sir?'

'Methinks we'll search your room first.'

Lowering my eyes in case he saw the triumph I felt, I said quickly 'Oh no! Surely there is no need for that.'

Still holding my hand that I tried to pull from his grasp, he called to the soldiers, 'Search the lady's bedchamber.'

Dragging my hand free, I turned to run up the stairs. My body obeyed me clumsily and where I but sought to delay him, I found instead that my toe caught in the hem of my gown and, before I could save myself or the Captain catch me, I tumbled heavily down the stairs to lie in a crumpled heap at the bottom.

The fall had been a heavy one and I lay for a moment while the Great Hall whirled madly about my head. As my senses cleared, a pair of strange black boots came into my line of vision as I lay with my cheek against the cold wooden floor. The Parliamentarian knelt on one knee beside me and touched my shoulder. As he lifted me, pain stabbed through my body and I clutched my stomach.

'The babe,' I cried, feeling sweat break out on my forehead. ''Tis too soon.'

'Lie still,' he said, 'and I'll send for your woman.' His tone was anxious and I knew that, however involuntarily, I'd diverted his thoughts for the moment. Pain hit again and I writhed in his arms, my fingers clutching at his. His fingers were warm and hard and turned in my grip to hold my hand in a comforting grasp. 'In one minute, when you feel better, I will carry you to your chamber; the maid awaits you there.'

And I realised that orders had been given while I lay there unaware of anything but the possibility of losing the baby I carried beneath my heart. After a while, whether minutes or hours I could not say, I was aware of lying on a bed while Meg tended me, and much later I awoke in the daylight to the bitter realisation that my body was my own again, no smaller heart beat with mine. As I turned my head into the pillow and swallowed salt tears, Meg rose from beside the fire and held a cup to my lips.

'Ashley?' I asked weakly. I had no need to ask after my unborn child.

'So, 'twas him as caused all the trouble,' she said grimly as I drank thirstily. 'Well he's safe away. They found the tunnel but no-one was there.'

'Have they gone?'

89

'Aye. The captain sent a man for our apothecary but much good he'll do. 'Tis over and done with.'

And so my poor little babe's epitaph was spoken 'over and done with', and he'd never lived a moment or seen the light of day. I thought my cup of sorrows was full but the gods had not yet done with me or Summer Ho.

CHAPTER EIGHT

While all this had been happening to me, Harry had had his own adventures, relieving Newark with Prince Rupert, and then marching back to Oxford. I had wondered if I'd see him then, and was still unsure of my reception of him, having told him neither of the girl, Betty, or the loss of our own baby. However, I was saved from making excuses or explanations; the Prince marched to York and all I saw of my husband was a hastily scrawled note and a pair of green silk shoes sent by a carrier.

Later came news of the defeat at Marston Moor and, in the same letter, I first heard the name 'Ironsides' that was coined by Prince Rupert for the seemingly invincible Parliament forces and that came to be so feared thereafter. But just when our spirits were at their lowest came reports of Royalist victories in the West Country. In early September the Roundhead infantry surrendered at Lostwithiel, and the King's party dared to hope again.

Most of the servants at Summer Ho had drifted away and who could blame them? What man wanted to be away from his home in such desperate times and where should a maid be but with her own family? Meg and I did our best to refill the store cupboard with preserves and jams, while faithful Tom Holwell forgot his age and worked like a youth in the first strength of his manhood to provide hay and fodder for the house cow and the horses.

Both Mally and little Hal seemed to grow while we looked at them, and my evenings and any spare moment were taken up by sewing tiny garments for them.

The year slowly changed to autumn and I realised that soon the summer campaign would be over and Harry home again. Knowing that I must soon face the prospect of acknowledging the baby's parentage, I hugged him closer on my lap and sighed as I looked down at Mally playing happily on the floor at my feet. Hal seemed to have filled the space left by the loss of my own child and I knew that I could never part with him. He would have to be brought up as part of my household and I knew I had the task of persuading Harry that this was so. Usually in such cases the child would be placed with some farmer or other local family to be brought up and the natural father, while seeing him occasionally, would pay for his keep and schooling but, apart from that, he would have little or no contact with his real family. I wanted better than this for Hal and would do my best to see that his birth did not tell against him.

Absorbed by my thoughts, I gradually became aware that a sound had grown in the quiet room. Above the baby's prattle came the sound of horses, not excited galloping but slow plodding hoofs that carried some heavy burden. Meeting Meg's eyes I arose and, handing her the baby, hurried to the window.

For a moment I could see nothing because of the surrounding wall and gatehouse, and then a Parliament soldier appeared in the archway and, behind him, a farm wagon. One glance told me that there was a figure on it, lying still and swathed in a cloak. With a heart that had suddenly turned to stone and seemed to fill my chest with pain so that I gasped for breath, I turned with a smothered exclamation and ran out of the room.

The cortège had reached the steps by the time I flung open the main door and was confronted by Captain Everton, his hand raised to knock.

Astounded, I gazed at him blankly and then my eyes, going beyond his redcoated shoulders, saw my husband's personal servant hovering around the still form on the floor of the wagon.

'Harry!' I gasped in a soundless whisper and,

brushing past the Roundhead, ran down the steps.

It was Harry, but so limp and pale that I hardly recognised him and suddenly realised how much his liveliness and vigour contributed to his character.

Afraid to touch him, afraid of what I might find or do with a heedless movement, I looked back over my shoulder to the silent figure on the steps. Slowly he joined me and, for a few seconds, stood looking down at me with an unreadable expression in his eyes, then he said quite gently, 'Have you someone to help?'

'There's Tom,' I answered, gesturing to the steward who had heard the commotion and come to see the cause. 'And there's the stable boy somewhere.'

He touched my shoulder in a fleeting gesture. 'Go and make ready a bed and we'll make shift to carry him there.'

By the time I heard their labouring footsteps on the stairs I had turned back the covers on my bed and spread an old sheet over all to protect them from Harry's soiled clothes and muddy boots. Unwrapping the cloak I sighed with relief when no gaping, bloody wound was revealed, but when I would have removed his boots a hand stayed me.

'I fear 'tis his back and, in such cases, it's best to move them as little as possible.' When I looked at him blankly, he went on, 'Believe me, I've seen such hurts before.'

'You mean his spine is broke?' I asked through dry lips.

Instead of answering my question, he said, 'His horse fell on him.'

'Poor Blackboy,' I whispered touching Harry's cold hand and watching the soldier's deft hands as they gently cut away the clothing from my husband's limp body.

It was not until we had washed him and sent for an apothecary that I had time to wonder how Captain Everton came to bring Harry home.

'His man was there and told me his name,' he answered briefly, swinging away from the bed. Standing beside the window, looking out at the rapidly darkening garden, he went on. 'I may as well tell you; there had been a battle at Newbury and I was pursuing him. His horse put a foot in a pothole and pitched over, breaking his own neck and pinning your husband to the ground.'

'My ... thanks for bringing him home.'

He turned to face me across the bed. 'I had to choose, and I only hope I chose aright. Bringing him here and jolting him over the roads may have injured his back anew, but to have left him to the tender mercies of the local populace, when he desperately needed much care...'

Silence fell in the darkening room and, after a while, I took a taper from the mantleshelf and began to light the candles. A golden glow filled the chamber with illusory comfort and, bending over the still figure on the bed, I smoothed back the hair from Harry's face and prayed that the surgeon would come soon.

Leaving Tom Holwell watching beside his master, I took Captain Everton downstairs for a much needed meal. He ate sparingly and with little interest and I could see that his greatest need was for rest.

'Will you stay the night?' I asked.

He shook his head. 'My girls have need of me. I must ride home.'

'I have seen you so often and yet I have no idea where is your home?'

He pushed a piece of bread round his plate with his finger and did not look at me. 'When I say "home" 'tis no more than a term. My house was burned to the ground at the beginning of this summer, and now my children are with their aunt, my wife's kinswoman.'

'I'm sorry, was it ...?'

'No, not the war, a mere accident I understand.'

'I see. And your wife? I believe the last time we met she was about to lie in?'

He was suddenly still and then, giving the bread a final push to the side of his plate, leaned back in his chair. 'She died in childbed,' he answered briefly.

I could only say inadequately again, 'I'm sorry,' and try to turn his mind to happier thoughts. 'Tell me about your children, girls I think you said?'

'Bess is nine and Jennet two years younger. I fear they have taken the loss of their mother and home badly. My kinswoman is elderly and set in her ways. 'Tis hard for her to look after children as it is for them to be there. It is a situation that cannot be long endured.'

'You have not seen them since?'

'This will be the first time. You will understand why I can't linger.'

'You have my most grateful thanks for delaying this long…'

I was interrupted by a scratching at the door as Meg brought the children to say their 'Goodnights', Hal a sleepy bundle in her arms and Mally clinging silently to her skirts as is her wont when strangers are near.

As I bent over him, Hal blew a bubble with milkladen breath and suddenly opened his bright blue eyes. I could have been looking down at my husband and I caught my breath with pain as I dropped a kiss on his rounded cheek before turning to my little Mally and, sweeping her up in my arms, I hugged and kissed her, taking comfort from the feel of her firm little body before setting her back on her feet and, gathering her leading strings that hung from her shoulders, handed them back into Meg's capable hands.

There was silence for a few minutes after the door closed behind them and then Captain Everton stirred and said,

'Two fine children, mistress. The boy is the image of his father.'

'Yes ... he's ...' Closing my eyes, I bit my lip, realising that he thought Hal was the baby I'd lost. With an effort, keeping my voice steady, I said hastily, 'He's a golden boy, and my little Mally will be a brown girl like me.'

'An she favours her mother it will be no hardship.'

I smiled my thanks for the compliment and, as he rose, stood up also.

'Again my thanks for your care of my husband, and may I hope that you find your daughters' circumstance better than you have cause to suppose?'

'May I express the hope that if we meet again 'twill be under happier auspices?' he said formally, bowing over my hand.

In a short while I heard his horse clatter under the gatehouse and, picking up my skirts, ran back to my bedchamber. Tom Holwell rose from beside the bed as I entered and I looked at him in interrogation.

'He stirred a few minutes since and almost opened his eyes.'

'Oh, Tom, how do you think he is?'

'I could like it better if he came out of this stupor.'

'But there's no wound ... surely 'tis none so bad,' I cried, frightened by his grave tone, but he would only say the surgeon would know, and so I had to curb my worry and wait

97

impatiently for the sounds of his arrival.

My good steward and I divided the night between us and at last, just after dawn, Harry stirred. I had gone to the window and drawn the curtains on a world as grey and miserable as I felt, when I heard a movement behind me and turned to see him move weakly against his pillows.

'Harry!' I cried and ran to the side of the bed. His head turned slowly and bright blue eyes stared up at me.

'Anne?' he asked weakly. 'Anne—but I ...'

'You're home and safe,' I reassured him quickly, 'with nothing to bother you,' and at that moment the surgeon from Alton arrived.

Dr Blake was small and rotund with a manner that exuded kindness and confidence. At once I knew I could trust him and that he was not a quack who would palm me off with magical verse and useless pills.

He examined Harry in silence, treating him at once like a kindly uncle and a strict schoolmaster. Harry, I was relieved to see, though very weak, gave no signs of relapsing again into unconsciousness. When the doctor had finished, he settled him back against the pillows with womanly kindness and, turning to me, took my elbow and led me from the room.

'It's bad?' I said slowly when I had poured him wine and settled him on the settle in the hall.

Looking at me over the rim of his glass, he

did not answer but asked instead,

'Your husband, I take it, is an active man?'

I nodded and waited, while my heart began to beat hard and fast against my ribs.

'Of course in these cases, one can never tell. I have seen men recover completely and others...'

'And others?'

'Prognosis has not been so good.'

'I pray you, sir, tell me. The worst I must bear, but uncertainty will break me.'

He drained his glass and set it down. A shaft of autumn sunlight played across the table and, even now, I can remember how the particles of dust danced in its light.

'Very well, madam. The degree of paralysis I have been able to detect is confined to his lower limbs. I cannot at this moment say how final my diagnosis must be, but I fear the prognosis must be ... poor!'

Abruptly I sat down, while the world swung around and finally settled again. 'You mean he is ... *paralysed*?'

'I do, but you must take hope that in these cases nothing is final. No-one can tell how badly or how little the spinal cord is damaged. At this stage, bruises or severance could cause much the same symptoms. You must remember, madam, that we are all in God's hands. I would suggest, however, that you maintain as bright and hopeful a demeanour as possible. Much must depend upon *your* outlook. Cheer him, urge him to effort and, above all, do not let him give up hope. Use your discretion about telling him; for the first few weeks I would suggest a little subterfuge, at least until he is stronger.'

'My thanks,' I said automatically, trying to take in what his diagnosis would mean. 'Will you call again?'

He paused at the door and then said, without looking back, and I realised that it was pain for his words, not indifference, that made him behave so. 'Unless you send for me, there will be no need.'

And I knew with sickening finality that Harry would never walk again.

CHAPTER NINE

The next weeks were spent in the sickroom. Harry did not retain consciousness for long, soon after the doctor had left he developed a burning fever. However, I was not unprepared for this, Dr Blake having suggested that it would be a normal course of his illness and having left some drops to be administered. For days Harry raved in delirium and during the time he tossed in nightmares, I listened to his wild voice and realised the full horrors of war. His back gave him much pain and, during that time, he begged me, like a child, for relief. After a while he grew quieter and seemed sunk in stupor, taking interest in nothing, not even rousing to take food. It was not until after Christmas that he opened his eyes and knew me. I was nursing Hal at the time and I saw Harry's eyes go to the child.

'You never told me,' he murmured weakly and I had to bend near him.

'About what?'

'The boy. What have you named him?'

Nonplussed I stared at him. Having never told him before, how could I tell him now? At last my lips moved of their own volition. 'Harry,' I answered.

He made a weak gesture and knowing he wanted to take my hand, I put mine in his. 'So, we have a son,' he said. 'I've ever had a mind for a son.'

I opened my mouth, but closed it again, with the words still unsaid, knowing that now was not the time. And so Harry accepted little Hal as his son, without questioning who his mother might be.

News of the war came to us slowly now with no man at the battlefield to keep us acquainted. Sometime in February we heard that the Parliament forces had formed themselves into what they called the New Model Army and that Fairfax, a north country gentleman much heard of during the wars, was to command it. Harry showed a little interest when I brought him Lord Holt's letter and, seeing him deep in discussion with Tom Holwell over what it might portend, I ventured to steal away from the sickroom and avail myself of the better weather to wander out into the air for a few minutes.

Since Harry's arrival in November, I had hardly ventured outside the house. The winter snows had passed me by almost unknowing and now I found a soft wind heralding spring blowing in the garden and here and there, amid the dark, wet earth, showed small green spikes as early flowers dared to show their leaves. The gravel of the Elizabeth Walk scrunched beneath my pattens and I knew that while the winter garden showed little sign of the neglect it suffered, come the spring and summer and we would see all too clearly the lack of men to weed and plant.

The sweet wind lifted my hair away from my forehead and, on impulse, I pulled out the pins securing my bun and shook my hair free. It tumbled down and with both hands I ran my fingers threw it and lifted it away from my scalp. At that moment I longed for a gallop on Mab such as I had not known for months. Knowing I could not leave Harry for long, I turned back to the house and saw Mally emerge from the door. Seeing me, she shrieked with delight and hurled herself down the steps and into my arms.

'Show, show!' she demanded, obviously remembering the summer when I had carried her to see the treasures of the garden and, obediently, I turned about, taking her to see where the green daffodil leaves were beginning to show and where some bright moss made a soft damp carpet as it crept over a flagstoned path.

Suddenly the thin winter sun vanished as a dark cloud dashed up to cover the sky. Catching up Mally in my arms, I ran with her to the house, arriving in the Great Hall just as the rain beat fiercely against the windows. The steward, who was coming downstairs, said that Harry wanted me and, without setting the child down, I ran up to his room still windblown and with the first raindrops on my cloak.

'What did you want?' I began, but stopped, seeing Harry's eyes upon me with a strange expression in their depths.

'I can smell the wind upon you,' he said hungrily and I knew how he chaffed against his weak and useless body.

'See, here is your little daughter come to keep you company,' I said hastily to change the subject, and put her to kneel in a chair beside the bed.

He touched her hair and smiled and, for a while, she prattled happily to him but, after a while, lost interest and scrambled down to go and stare out of the window at the rain.

Taking up my sewing, I settled myself in the chair she had vacated. 'What think you of this New Army we hear of?' I asked, searching for my needle.

He turned restlessly against the pillow and frowned. 'They've chosen their two most able men to lead it; Essex has gone to the wall and now Tom Fairfax and Cromwell come forward. Rupert often said they were men to watch. Methinks, with their army better trained and equipped than ever before, they will prove invincible.'

'You mean—we are lost?'

'Aye. 'Tis now that the King needs every man and here I am—tied by the tail like a captive hare.' Suddenly his thin hand reached out and seized my wrist, holding it aloft with the needle poised for a stitch. 'Tell me, Anne,' he said urgently, *'tell me*, will I ever walk again?'

I looked down at his hand, thinking how quickly it had grown pale. Only a few months ago that pallid slim hand had been hard and brown. 'Dr Blake says we must be patient— healing of an injury such as yours must take time.'

Giving my wrist an impatient shake, he released me. 'My legs feel nothing—from the hips down I am like a dead man.' Suddenly he reached down as far as he could and struck his legs a violent blow. 'There—and I felt nothing I tell you,' he cried.

I caught his hand as he raised it for another blow and carried it to my chest. 'Time, Harry, give them time. When the summer comes, with the better weather, you will feel a difference.'

His fingers twisted in mine. 'Will I Anne—
will I?' he asked, and over our joined hands our
eyes met and asked the question that neither of
us could voice.

As the days went by he grew stronger and by
mid February could sit up, propped by a
mound of pillows. About this time he had a
return of sensation in his lower body which
made the task of nursing him easier. But
although our spirits and hopes rose, his legs
remained dead and useless with no sign of life
returning to them. At first he knew hope but, as
time went on, his hopes died and he grew more
despairing, raging against fate for whole days
at a time, wondering aloud why he could not
have been killed in battle and ranting against
the man who had brought him home and not
left him to die. Death was very much on his
mind and, during this period, I spent much of
my time devising ways to distract him.

During one such day when he had been more
than usually despondent, I recalled to mind a
pair of flintlock pistols that he had brought
back from Germany and had carried into
battle with him. It took his manservant only a
few minutes to find them but when I would
have taken them he stopped me. I studied the
man's hangdog expression and, remembering
that he had seemed unhappy for some time,
asked him what ailed him.

''Tis the master,' he answered at last

clutching the pistols to his narrow chest and, staring at the toes of his boots, 'I can't abide to see him like this.'

'None of us can,' I reminded him.

At that he looked up and I saw the real misery in his eyes. 'I've been with him many a year. I looked after him and young Sir Ashley when they were on the Grand Tour; many's the time I've waited up to undress him and I've lost count of the meals I've scavenged for him during the war, but I can't bear to see him lying there so still and desperate. 'Twould have been better fate if he'd been killed.'

'You want to go then?'

'If it please you. My heart bleeds, but I've never been good in illness; there's something about helpless men that unsettles me. Some could nurse and love him still but my Master Harry was a fine strong boisterous lad. To see him a helpless cripple turns my heart to water.'

Looking at the uncomfortable man as he tried to justify himself to me, I sighed, wishing that we all could dismiss our duties so easily. 'Come to me this evening and I'll try to find some money in payment for your services. You had best say you've had a message recalling you home. Make your own excuses but, I charge you, hide the real reason.' And, snatching up the pistols, I ran from the room.

When I entered his bedchamber, Harry was lying listlessly gazing out of the window. We had pulled the great fourposter nearer the casement but the view seemed to afford him little amusement.

'Your man says that these are in need of oiling,' I said, laying the pistols across his knees, 'and, knowing that none but you may touch your weapons, I've brought your rag and linseed oil.'

For a while he looked at them, then touched the chased stocks with one finger. 'They saved my life, do you know Anne?' he said suddenly. 'We'd met in a skirmish, the Rebels outnumbering us and, in the fray, I lost my sword. A great fellow with a black eyeshade came at me—I'll never forget him as long as I live. He seemed a veritable giant and his face was covered in the most verdant beard I'd ever seen. For a moment I was helpless and then, recalling my pistols that I'd loaded and primed before we set out, I tore them from my sash pocket and fired them both full at my assailant.'

'What happened?'

'Must have killed him for he fell off his horse—and then we were through and away with Ashley laughing all the way back into camp.' A half smile of recollection curved his mouth and I waited, taut with suspense before, quite naturally, he took up the materials in his long fingers and began to clean the guns.

'Do you know how to load?' he asked casually.

'My father taught me but 'tis many years

107

since I did so, I've almost forgot.'

'Find the materials and I'll refresh your memory.' It was the work of seconds to find the powder and balls which had all been lying near. Heedless of any danger, I laid them all on the bed and stood near watching Harry at work. When he had finished, I had to imitate his actions until he was satisfied, and then the guns were unloaded and put away.

'But tomorrow, Anne, we'll open the window and set up a target in the courtyard. You shall practise until you can beat me.'

With pleasure I noted the light back in his voice and hoped his interest would last, but the next day his back pained him making him fretful and short tempered.

When he missed the target for the second time and threw down his pistol declaring that the sooner I was proficient the better, as he would never be able to defend his home, I knew that I must take care never to hit at what I aimed.

Quite suddenly he seemed to give up all hope, where a few weeks ago he had been able to sit up and even be lifted out of bed and spend a while in a chair, now he could only lie prone. His flesh seemed to fall away while I looked at him and, search my books how I would for samples and medicines, nothing I could make improved him. Day by day I had to stand by and see him steadily becoming more despondent and depressed until he would lie still and silent for hours.

Thinking to interest him, I had brought the children into his bedchamber but, after a while, seeing that their chatter and movement irritated him, I shooed them from the room.

'Is your back painful?' I asked, going to fetch the little bottle of laudanum from the high cupboard where I kept it. As I poured the liquid into a spoon, I saw Harry's eyes upon my hands with a peculiar hungry expression. When he had taken the medicine and I had stoppered the bottle and would have put it away, he held my wrist with thin fingers that surprised me with their strength.

'Leave it, Anne, I might have need of it later.'

His intense tone startled me and, looking down into his pleading blue eyes, I read in their depths a message that took me several moments to understand and, when I did, I drew back from the bed clutching the bottle to me and shaking my head.

'No! no!' I whispered, through suddenly dry lips. 'Oh Harry, not *that*!'

His eyes gleamed feverishly. 'Why not?' he questioned. ''Tis my life and—I have done with it.' There was such bitterness in his voice that the tears started to my eyes. 'I had thought that you loved me,' he went on, drawing me gently, insidiously to him. 'Can you wish me to live like this—a half dead, useless body? Anne, *Anne*, an you love me you will give me

109

this chance.'

Close against him for the first time in months, held tight in his arms, and with his heart beating under my ear, I reacted automatically and turned my face to his, straining my body against his. His mouth moved hungrily against mine and, with a muttered groan, he crushed me to him. For a moment I lay in a haze of remembered passion and then, quite suddenly, he released me and turned his head against the pillows, while his body shook with half stifled sobs.

'Harry?' I said timidly, laying a gentle hand on his arm. Leaning across the great bed, I took his head between my hands and turned him to look at me. 'Hold me—love me,' I pleaded. ''Tis so long and we can still find joy together.'

With a violent gesture he struck at me, catching my shoulder and half tumbling me from the bed.

'Leave me, leave me,' he shouted, his eyes wild and his voice almost inarticulate with emotion. 'God help me, I have no need of you. Don't you understand or must I say I am but half a man.'

His bitter words hung in the air. A log crackled and spat in the fireplace, while I stared at him. Whatever I had expected it was not this. I should have known, guessed but, never having nursed a paralysed man before, nothing had prepared me for this event.

'Go, go!' he shrieked, seeming beside himself and thrashing about the bed. 'Go, Anne, or I will find the strength to drag myself across the floor and hurl myself from the window—I swear it.'

With an effort that corded his throat and left his voice hoarse, he spoke with a semblance of calm. For a second I had a horrific vision of him crawling across the wooden boards like an injured beetle that kindly folks stamped on to put it out of its misery and then, as he made a movement to pull himself to the side of the bed, voice and movement returned to me and I tried to speak calmly.

'I'll go—if that's what you really want,' I said, 'but only because you ask me to. Not because I love you the less. There's more to love than two bodies expressing it physically. If you would hold me, kiss me, I would be very happy.' I took a tentative step forward and touched the sleeve of his nightshirt. 'Let me stay,' I pleaded.

As if I had struck him, he recoiled and thrust my arm away. 'Pity!' he spat at me, 'I'll have none of your pity. Go and see to your brats—you'll have no more from me. Doubtless you think you have me safe tied by my coat tails for the rest of my life but you forget, I have my memories to live on. You couldn't count the women I've loved. Didst think I'd live like a monk away from you? I've enjoyed every day—and night—of this war, especially the nights...'

Unable to bear listening to more, I clapped my hands over my ears and, blinded by stinging tears, ran from the room but, even in my haste, remembering to pick up the pistols and carry them with me. All that day Harry's words echoed in my ears. Even at his most indifferent he had never been cruel before. His words had a vicious deliberate ring to them as though he had forced himself to say them.

It was not until the early hours of the morning that I realised what he had done. Sitting up alert and awake, my brain icily cool, I clearly remembered leaving the bottle of laudanum on the table beside his bed as he had manœuvred me into doing.

When I opened the door, his chamber was in darkness but a shaft of moonlight fell across the bed and the man lying against the pillows. For a moment I thought I was too late and then Harry opened his eyes and smiled at me.

'I'm glad you came,' he said, so slowly and softly that I could hardly hear him. 'I wanted you, Anne.'

CHAPTER TEN

And so they found us in the morning, the living and the dead, clasped in each other's arms.

'Come away, mistress,' said that good old

man Tom Holwell, not attempting to hide the tears in his eyes and, reluctantly, I laid down my heavy burden that I had held so long.

With soft murmurs and gentle hands, Meg urged me out of the room and back to my own. Refusing to return to bed, I allowed her to dress me, and it was not until I was alone again that I found that all this while I had been clasping the little glass bottle that had once held laudanum. My fingers were numb with the intensity of my grip and, as I stared down, the early spring sunshine broke through the scudding clouds and, finding its way into my chamber, drew sparks of fire from the cutglass in my hand. Dazzled and half blinded, but still dry eyed and frozen in my grief, I stumbled to the table and pushed the bottle among the jars holding my cosmetics.

Slowly the hours wore away and I swear that I lived a lifetime alone in my room for I would see no-one, while I went over and over the events of the previous day. That Harry had determined to take his own life, I had no doubt, but was forced to search my conscience at his manner of achieving it. Knowing that he had intended to drive me from him, in a flood of emotion, in the hopes that I would leave the laudanum behind, I still blamed myself for not taking it with me. All my concentration on the pistols, I had forgotten the deadly drops I left beside the bed and knew that I would ever wonder, if only he had been denied the means, whether another day would have found him of a different mind.

Finding no comfort in the children, Meg brought in the hopes that they might soothe me, I sent them away and paced the floor like a wild creature that one sees in a cage. Unable to stay still for more than a moment, with my thoughts in a turmoil and my mind afire, I walked from the fire to each peace of furniture, touching and moving familiar things, and yet feeling and recognising nothing.

When I first heard the clatter of hoofbeats I have no idea but, quite suddenly, the sound impinged on my brain and, recognising it for what it was, I ran to the window, for one wild moment believing that the previous events had been a nightmare and now I would awake to find Harry riding under the archway.

The red sleeves, buff coats and shining pot helmets made me catch my breath with surprise. For a moment I stared with my face close against the diamond panes of the casement, then I *knew*—these were the men that killed my husband. Not with sword out or pistol shot, but just as surely. In that second as they vanished from sight on the road, and I knew that next I would see them emerging from under the gatehouse, I knew what I must do.

The pistols were ready to hand, still loaded as I had left them last night, by the time the first horse showed his head under the arch, my window was open and I was waiting to take aim, my hands steady for the first time in hours.

The sound of the shot filled the room as Meg burst in. Smoke and the smell of powder eddied around us as she rushed forward and pulled me away from the casement.

'What have you done?' she cried. 'Oh, what have you done?'

'Taken a life in return for my husband,' I said coldly, letting the pistol fall to the floor.

''Tis foolishness—they'll fire the house for sure now!' The mists cleared from my mind and I realised what I had done. For a second I met her frightened gaze and then turned and ran from the room, thinking if only I could explain to them, they would understand; even Roundheads were men and would understand a woman's distress. My calm and hope lasted until I came out onto the steps leading from the courtyard and there at the bottom lay the body of Tom Holwell, his old grey head stained with blood, one frail hand still holding an ancient battleaxe he had taken from the wall to defend Summer Ho.

Slowly my eyes moved from his pathetic remains to the man who stood beside him, past the huge black jackboots and the heavy skirts of the buff coat, lingering a moment on the vivid orange sash that slanted across his breastplate and then upwards over the wide linen collar to the grim implacable face under the smooth steel helmet.

The faceguard made curious shadows but, even so, I recognised Captain Everton and read in his cold expression no sign of mercy.

'My Cornet lies near death,' he spoke in a clipped manner, his lips scarce moving. 'And for that the house and its contents shall burn—and you, Mistress Summer, shall watch until the last ember lies cold.'

For the rest of that terrible day I watched Summer Ho destroyed, or so Meg tells me for, by God's Grace, I remember little.

The soldiers took me and made me stand in the courtyard, and all around was bustle as they searched the house taking all that might be of use to them, the few of my servants that remained were allowed to remove nothing.

After a while the acrid stench of smoke came to my nostrils and the Parliamentarians ran from the door as flames appeared at the upper windows.

Meg tells me that Captain Everton learned of Harry's body from his men, but by then the house was well alight and it was not possible to remove him. She says the Roundhead spoke to me at the time but I have no recollection of this.

I can remember the small, ordinary things; my legs aching from standing so long, hands brushing a smouldering spark from the skirt of my gown, but of the actual conflagration I remember little except staring upwards as the fire devoured the Queen's Chamber, the tears slid down my cheeks, and then feeling the sharp cobbles beneath my knees as the strength left my legs.

Meg took her courage then and begged that she might take me away but, after a glance at his wounded Cornet, Captain Everton refused. A high-backed chair, salvaged from the Great Hall was brought and I was lifted into it, and so I sat in state to see the end of my home.

Meg says that after the fire had done its work and died down, the Captain strode over to us and stood regarding me as he pulled on his great gauntleted gloves.

'See to your mistress,' he commanded my poor faithful Meg, as though she would have done anything else and, climbing into the saddle of his horse, gave orders to his troop and they rode away, leaving desolation and a group of frightened women and children behind them.

Meg was a staunch friend during the next few days; by the time I had recovered my senses, she had established us in the tiny chamber belonging to the gatehouse, rummaged through the ruins and found and rescued several useful items, salvaged some food from what remained of the kitchens and set about making our shelter habitable.

'What of Tom Holwell?' I asked. 'We can't leave him.'

'He's not on the steps; the soldiers saw to him.'

Something in her tone made me look at her. 'They ...?'

'They put him in the fire,' she answered bluntly. 'Now don't go fretting yourself; it's what he would have wanted hisself. He loved Summer Ho and to see it burned down as well as losing the master would have been more than he could bear.'

'I think 'tis more than I can bear,' and the weak tears came.

'Never say so,' her voice was brisk but her eyes were kind. 'You've the babes to think of and there's much to do. There's just the two of us you know. The few that were left have all gone now.'

'If only poor Tom were here—to have been killed like that! They must have struck him down without giving him a chance to defend himself.'

'He weren't touched.'

'But I saw the blood on him myself.'

'I were watching. He took down the battleaxe, rushed to the door and, as he stood on the step defying the soldiers like, he suddenly fell as if poleaxed, but I swear no-one touched him. He must have struck his head as he fell.'

'Poor man, we could do with him now.'

'You have me, Miss Anne, we'll manage,' she stated with sturdy self-confidence.

She proved her worth in the days that followed. Having been born on a farm, she was competent and adaptable. How I and the children would have managed without her I cannot say but, within days, she had cleared the gatehouse of the dirt and rubbish that had accumulated during the years it had not been used, collected straw from the burned stables and even set up a modest store cupboard with the remains of food from the kitchens. Clothes and bedding were obviously going to be a necessity. Meg had snatched up a change of linen for little Hal, but, apart from that, none of us had more clothes than those we wore.

Summer Ho had been gutted, standing a gaunt blackened ruin, its walls open to the sky. Even if we had managed to climb to what had been the upper storeys, we would have found nothing for the hungry flames had done their work only too well; of furnishings and wooden fittings nothing was left, only the stonework had escaped being consumed. Resolutely putting aside all thoughts of my home as it had been, I turned my mind to ways of supplementing our scanty wardrobe and at last recalled ordering a box of materials, too good to be used as rags, to be put in one of the outhouses. The roofs of these had gone too but here the fire had not been so fierce and most of the contents had escaped.

We found the box, half hidden under fallen burned beams, and bore it back to the gate in triumph. Inside were several worn curtains, some patched sheets and, most treasured of all, three heavy dresses once worn by the kitchen wenches.

Lavender heads fell to the ground as I shook out the folds and the smell of remembered summers filled my nostrils. Meg unlaced me and I kicked aside the scorched, soiled, silken gown I'd worn ever since the morning of the fire. The dress felt heavy and coarse but smelt clean and could be easily made to fit me more closely.

So low were our spirits that such a small thing as finding the box sent us to bed in a mood of exultation but, by morning, a clearer frame of mind had returned and I knew that we faced a very real threat of starvation if we could not make provision for the winter. Therefore great was my joy when, on hearing a clatter of hoofs, I looked out of the tiny gatehouse window to see the home cow trotting into the yard and, close behind her like a following friend, came my beautiful Mab, ignoring the mud that covered her elegant legs and setting her neat hooves as precisely as if she had been carrying a Queen.

The cow would provide milk for the children and my sweet grey mare would provide the money we needed to set us up for the coming months. Heartsore at the thought of parting with her, I ran out and, pulling her head against my chest, caressed her gentle face.

There was no time to be lost and, as the next day was market in Alton, I set out early in the morning, leaving the children in Meg's care. Despite my fears, the journey was ease itself. Having ridden far afield in happier times, I knew the way for several miles and, when I came onto strange roads, there were many others, farmers and wives and many poor folk obviously heading for market, and I had only to follow my fellow travellers to find myself in the little town.

Here were more people than I had seen in a long time and, if one ignored the bullet holes in some walls and the damaged Church on its hill, reminiscent of the fierce battle that had taken place two years ago, there were few signs of war, apart from the soldiers who mingled with the crowd. Stalls lined the small square and at one end were gathered the animals to be sold. I walked Mab to join them and then slid from her back, twisted her reins over my arm and stood by her side to wait for a buyer.

The armies, with their ever present need for mounts, had created a shortage of horses, and many people eyed Mab, but none with so great an interest as one man. I noticed him in particular because one sleeve hung empty and was tucked into his sword belt. Seeing me watching him, he smiled ruefully and moved off.

The day drew on, and the porrage I had eaten for breakfast seemed a long time ago, but with no money in my pocket I could buy nothing until Mab was sold. Some soldiers stopped to look at her but she was not up to a man's weight and they moved on. At last, when I was beginning to despair of making a sale, a large man stopped in front of me and, without a word, opened Mab's mouth to examine her teeth.

He was red-faced and just beginning to run to fat. The clothes he wore proclaimed him a wealthy farmer, and I wondered how he had managed to keep his money during the last years.

Still without a word to me, he lifted Mab's foreleg and looked at the hoof, then proceeded to feel her shoulders and legs.

'She's not up to your weight!' I said sharply, more to remind him of my presence than because I really thought he intended to ride her.

'I know it,' he answered briefly, favouring me with a disinterested glance, and I saw that his eyes were small and shrewd in his rosy face. 'I breed them—a good mare's hard to come by.'

Suddenly I knew that I disliked him. There had been no kindness in his hands as he touched Mab and the thought of him breeding foal after foal on her until she was worn-out was more than I could bear.

'She's not for sale,' I said suddenly, and pulled the reins so that Mab jerked her head free from his hand.

His little eyes narrowed until they were mere

slits. 'What do you mean? Why are you standing here if she's not to be sold?'

'I've altered my mind! Be so good as to leave us.'

His face altered at my tone; he examined me more closely and, as he took in my dress and general appearance, a cunning expression gleamed in his eyes. 'Hoity toity,' he replied. 'And who may you be, acting so high and mighty?'

Trying to ignore him, I turned my back and hid behind Mab's grey shoulder, but he dodged under her head and, putting a rough hand on my arm, turned me to face him.

'Come to that, how do I know the horse is yours to sell?' His eyes travelled over me, taking in my coarse servant's dress, the grubby lace of my shift, and my worn satin slippers. 'You don't look right,' he understated, 'and whoever heard of a *woman* selling horseflesh.'

'Let me go,' I said angrily, trying to twist free of his grasp, conscious of the dawning interest in the scene of the people nearby.

'I'll give you five pounds,' he said quietly, his face unpleasantly near mine and his fingers biting into my arm.

'No!' I cried, as his free hand was already reaching towards Mab's bridle.

He stared at me in surprise. 'I'll not go higher.'

'If you offered me a hundred pounds you'd still not have her,' I hissed, and stamped

123

heavily on his instep, jerking my arm free as his grip slackened.

'Then I'll call the soldiers,' the man shouted angrily, his face reddening unpleasantly, 'and they can settle this...'

'Can I be of help?' asked a quiet voice, and I turned to see the one-armed man standing behind me.

'This man is annoying me!'

The newcomer looked over the fat man. 'Farmer Noyse,' he said thoughtfully, and the other smiled ingratiatingly. 'I believe you have grown wealthy on selling horses to the Parliamentary forces—an you don't leave this lady alone I'll make it my duty to see that you never sell another there.'

The smile abruptly left the fat man's face. 'I offered a fair price,' he protested.

'She's not for sale and so I've told you,' I said.

'You see?' said my new friend. 'There is nothing to keep you from your other business,' and pointedly he turned his shoulder to smile down at me. 'Let me introduce myself. Ned Barlow at your service.'

'My name is Summer,' I answered, dropping a curtsey, 'and my thanks for your help.'

'I'm sorry to hear that the mare is not for sale. I had hoped to buy her for my son.'

'I just said that, having taken that man in abhorrence. If I don't sell her, we'll be in hard straits this winter.'

He examined her briefly and then said, 'I'll

give you ten pounds for her.'

'Done—provided I have the money quickly. I must buy some things before the market closes.'

He smiled as he pulled a knitted purse from his pocket and counted out ten golden coins into my hand. I laid my cheek against Mab's soft nose and then, thrusting the reins into his hands, walked quickly away before he should see the tears I was struggling to hold back.

While waiting to sell my sweet Mab I had mapped out the route I would take, and quickly I bought a meat pie and then walked from stall to stall assuaging my hunger in great bites. Soon my pocket was filled with a comb, a packet of needles and bundles of thread, then I bought the two most important things we needed—a barrel of salt and a smaller one of sugar—and turned my attention to the problem of getting home. The two barrels were in net bags and, twisting the ends about my hands, I walked towards the Winchester road, hoping to meet the waggoner there. But, upon reaching the inn where inquiries had told me he picked up passengers, I found the street empty and realised, with a sinking heart, that he must have left.

There was nothing to do but set off along the muddy road and hope that someone would take pity and offer me a seat in his waggon. The barrels steadily became heavier and the string handles cut into my hands. With each step I realised how tired I was and became more uncertain of reaching Summer Ho that night.

The spring dusk had started to fall, when I heard the sound of horses approaching quickly from behind me. A wave of apprehension filled me but, before I had time to climb up the bank and hide behind the hedge, the rider had drawn level with me and I saw, with startled amazement, that the grey horse he was leading was Mab. For a moment her new owner, Ned Barlow, and I regarded each other and then he leaned forward to say, 'I fear you missed your waggon—as I have an empty saddle can I offer you a ride?'

'Truly I grow weary but do our paths lie together? I go to Summer Ho.'

'I have heard of it and can take you several miles towards it until I leave the road.'

It was the work of minutes to tie my barrels to Mab's saddle and then climb up onto her familiar back. For a while we rode in silence and then my companion said, 'I've been thinking. I can hardly leave you upon the road with night coming on. Will you allow me to escort you to Summer Ho?'

''Tis out of your way,' I pointed out. 'I could not ask so much of a stranger.'

'We have Mab as a bond,' he smiled. ''Tis settled then. I'll see you home and then ride on.'

And so I rode home in state with a gentleman to escort me. Parting with Mab was not so bad as I had feared, feeling as I did, that Ned Barlow would be a kind master and give her all the things I was now unable to provide. It was almost dark when we reached Summer Ho and I watched my new friend ride off into the darkness before hurrying under the gatehouse.

CHAPTER ELEVEN

The spring that year was warm and, luckily, summer came early! We managed to buy a side of bacon and hang it in our chimney to smoke, and a sheep, some of which we salted down for future use and, eating part of it, we saved its fat for tallow to make rush lights. I had been down to the river to collect the reeds to strip and dip into the fat to make lights for the winter and was returning with my arms full, when I saw the waggon stop at the gatehouse and a woman alight, while a huge amount of trunks and packages were set down in the road beside her. By the time I reached her, the waggon had moved off and Lettice was staring at the gaunt shell of Summer Ho, her mouth and eyes agape with dismay. So intent was she that she failed to hear me approach and jumped when I touched her arm, turning quickly and then saying in a dazed way,

'Anne—Anne, why—what ever—?'

'The Rebels burned us,' I said briskly, eager to get her inside as she showed every sign of being about to swoon on the roadside.

Once inside our small living room, she looked about her blankly and it was not until Meg had brought her a mug of cold well water that her colour returned and intelligence returned to her eyes, and I knew she would ask the question I dreaded.

'But where is Granddame—and Harry?'

'Dame Allis died over a year ago—quite peacefully, of old age I suppose,' I answered as calmly as I was able, 'and Harry was wounded at the second battle of Newbury. Blackboy fell on him and he was paralysed ... he didn't wish to live.'

I expected tears and lamentations but, to my surprise, she remained quite calm and I realised that, during the time she had been away, she must have become inured to accidents and death.

'Poor Harry,' was all she said and, sighing, put back the cloak from her shoulders and I saw that she was heavy with child.

'Letty,' I asked slowly, knowing the answer already, 'why have you come back?'

'Ashley sent me,' she said simply, 'I am to bear his child and he sent me here.'

'And where is he?'

'Gone to France—'tis the King's business and of more import than any of mine. Never trust a man, Anne.' She spoke with sudden

128

bitterness. 'They'll take all that's offered and give nothing of themselves in return.'

'Did Ashley know you're pregnant?'

Letty glanced down at herself. 'Could he be unaware of it?' she asked wryly. ''Tis the reason I'm here.' Could Ashley encumber himself with a breeding woman and one liable to produce at any moment, when he needed to make all speed to France? He gave me money and sent me off with his man to Alton, where he put me on the waggon for Summer Ho.' She looked about the tiny dark room, crammed with all the paraphernalia for the needs of two women with two children. 'Neither he or I dreamed it would be like this,' Letty went on, adding thoughtfully, 'though 'tis better than having it sequestered I suppose!'

'Sequestered?' asked I, never having heard the word before.

'The Parliamentary forces take over the estate of a known Royalist and give it to one of their own as a sort of reward. Ashley's estates have been usurped by a nephew of General Cromwell—stolen would be a better word for it.'

'I see,' I said and, knowing of a reluctance to talk of Ashley and his doings, said hastily, 'but we must talk of you, Letty. Will you stay here? The house is uninhabitable, this is where we live and where you must bear the babe if you stay. We have the bare necessities and, as you see, no furniture or furnishings. The village is

129

almost depopulated and there is no-one to help us if things go wrong with you.'

Tears sprang to her eyes and she clutched the cloak more tightly about her. 'You frighten me!' she whimpered. 'You shouldn't talk so, with me in my condition. Things must be made easy for women when their time is near.'

'I would have you know the truth,' I answered patiently. 'Meg has tended me with my babes, and I will be here to help, but we have no-one else to call on should the need arise—no man—midwife, no old goodwife in the village.' Letty stared at me, her eyes so like paler versions of my husband's that my heart beat faster. 'You have changed, Anne, a while ago and you would not have talked so.'

I shrugged. 'Times change. I am older—and wiser—than I was a year ago. Much older and much wiser, Letty,' and I sighed for that other woman I had been. 'When is the babe due?'

'This week or next,' she said, not interested.

'Should you have travelled so near your time? Pray you have not hurt the child.' Standing up, I looked at her and then crossed the room to the window. ''Tis obvious you must stay here—we will do our best.'

And we did but, in spite of all our efforts, the baby died. I held him in my arms, a small mewing version of Ashley, the same black hair and, for a moment, the same dark eyes as he opened them and gazed at me in the second his soul left this world. We buried him in a corner of the graveyard beside the family chapel and, after that, Letty seemed to gain ground. Before she had been dull and weighed down with care, but once the child was gone she rapidly regained her health and spirits.

'What will you do?' I asked one day as we sat in a sunny corner of the courtyard, I with my sewing and Letty with her dreams.

'Do?' She considered, her head on one side. 'I've heard that Denzil is back at our home—methinks my place is there beside him.'

From her expression I knew that she had already considered the possibilities of such a move and I merely asked 'How do you intend to get there?'

'Ashley gave me a purse before he left. If I could get to Alton I could hire a coach from there.'

Rising, I folded the new shift for Mally that was almost finished. 'We shall have to wait for the waggon to go past, or hope that a traveller will call,' I said.

But with Letty's usual luck, a visitor who could help her called the very next day.

I was washing some clothes in a tub in the courtyard when Ned Barlow, accompanied by a tall boy on Mab, rode under the gatehouse. 'Goodmorrow,' he greeted me gravely. 'May I present my son, Tom?' and hastily the boy pulled his hat from his head and imitated his father as he bowed from the saddle. 'We rode over to let you see that Mab has settled in with

131

us—and my wife insisted that I bring a cheese with me.' In case my pride would not let me accept the gift, he went on hastily, 'She prides herself on her cheese-making and ever wishes new acquaintances to taste her products.'

'Pray give her my thanks—as you know, we have need of provisions at the moment. Meg is making some oatcakes; will you stay and eat with us?'

He hesitated and then nodded. 'That would be very pleasant,' he said, swinging out of the saddle, and I noticed how little the loss of his arm bothered him.

As we entered the room over the gate, Letty, who had been sitting rather disconsolately by the fire, looked up and visibly brightened at the sight of Ned Barlow.

'Prithee, make us known,' she said curtseying prettily, and I knew a moment's irritation that she should have contrived to look clean and fresh while I was hot and dishevelled from the washing. The fact that her clothes had been among the laundry only served to further my pang of anger.

Making the necessary introductions, I retired to the other side of the fire and helped Meg put the finishing touches to the oatcakes that were cooking on the griddle over the heat and filling the small room with their appetising smell.

Halved and with a slice of bacon between, they made an appetising meal. Letty ate with finicky care, making sure that Master Barlow should be aware that she was not used to using her hands and fingers. All the drink we had was water but that was from our well and clean and sweet, not like the brackish town water that none dare drink.

After the meal, he rose to go and I walked with him to the gardens where we had tethered the horses, his son running before to release them. We talked of many things. In spite of his sober clothes and staid manner, so different to the men I had been used to, I found him easy to talk with, but it was not until he was about to mount that I found the courage to ask him the favour that had been on my mind all the time of his visit.

As he put a foot in the stirrup, I tentatively touched his arm and then was at a loss for words. Pausing, he looked down at me and then, putting his foot to the ground, he tossed the reins to his son and, taking my arm, led me a few paces away to a stone seat against the wall.

'I think you wish to ask me something,' he said as we sat. 'Pray believe that if it lies in my power, I shall be honoured to do it for you.'

I smiled at his gallant words. 'You speak like a Cavalier—but believe me, if you could arrange my request for me I would be grateful. My sister-in-law wishes to go to Alton, once there she can hire a coach and drive to her home. At the moment there is no way of getting her to town.'

'I see your difficulty,' he said gravely, and considered for a moment. 'I believe I can help. I go to Alton myself next week; if she could be persuaded to trust herself to my care, she could ride with me and I will arrange the details of the coach for her.'

'You are very kind.'

'A neighbour cannot do less. Shall I bring Mab or would Lady Halt prefer to ride pillion?'

'Pillion,' I said hastily, thinking of Mab's tender mouth and Letty's impatient hands.

And so it was arranged. Ned Barlow called for her early one morning, her boxes were tied onto the packhorse and she set off with scarcely a wave or a backward look. Meg and I were glad to see her go; she had given us no help and her company had been depressing. Letty's character was not of the kind to thrive under adversity; to be gay and bright she needed to be happy and in lively company. However, once she had gone I found my own spirits lower than they had been since that dreadful day when Harry had died and Summer Ho burned to the ground. I suppose that with much to do during the previous months to provision us and make the gatehouse habitable, I had had no time to think or consider our position but now, with my little money spent and whatever could be salvaged taken from the house, time hung on my hands.

134

In spite of the company of Hal and Mally, who grew brown and merry with their new freedom, for Meg and I had neither the time nor ability to keep them in long skirts and stockings or to remove them from whatever dirt they managed to find, I found myself growing miserable spending long hours thinking of Harry and all that had been. In retrospect our marriage seemed to have grown happier and Harry even more dear—and at the back of my mind was a shadowy figure that I dared not even acknowledge I thought about. Ashley had gone out of my life forever I told myself firmly. To have sent his discarded mistress to me showed very plainly how he thought of me, and yet a tiny traitorous voice inside me whispered in my brain that, now I was a widow, the circumstances were different.

Meg and I made over the clothing Letty had left behind. Much of it was useless—silks and satins had little use in the life we led, and while soft material shoes could be worn during the dry summer, the winter mud would soon ruin them. Her shifts and petticoats we shared between us and what was old or torn we cut up for the ever growing children.

Mally was now an enchanting two year old, prattling happily in her own language or attempting her version of our adult talk, and little Hal at eighteen months was the image of a miniature of Harry at the same age, that had laid on the table beside Dame Allis' bed. In spite of being bottlefed, he was a strong sturdy child showing no signs of the deprivation he had suffered from lack of mother's milk, and I can only suppose he never realised his lack for he accepted me as his mother. Mally thought of him as her brother and I swear that sometimes I almost believed that he was the babe I had lost the night I hid Ashley from the Roundheads.

The war had grown very quiet in this part of Hampshire. We heard from Ned Barlow that Cromwell was now Lt. General of the New Model Army and that victories were commonplace with his determination and the well-trained and armed troops under his command. It was obvious to all of us that now a complete Parliamentary victory was only months away and that soon the Monarchy, as we knew it, would cease to exist. To me, in what was left of Summer Ho, it all seemed very far away, and what fruit to try and preserve with our small amount of sugar and what meat to salt away was of much more import but quite soon Cromwell's long fingers were to reach out and disturb our tight little world in a manner that was both surprising and unpleasant.

CHAPTER TWELVE

Soon after Summer Ho had been destroyed, I thought of the Home Farm standing empty and, thinking that it would suit us better than the cramped gatehouse, determined to walk there and take stock of it, only to find that a tribe of tinkers had lodged themselves there. Obviously comfortable and settled for the moment, they showed no signs of being prepared to move and I, deciding that discretion would rule the day, left them in possession. However, early in July, I decided to see if they were still ensconced and walked across the Home Park towards the old house.

Long before I arrived, the noise of children playing and people shouting told me that they were still there and, taking refuge behind some leafy bushes, I spied out at them. Hordes of children and several men and women were busy about the yard, well-kept horses grazed in the field nearby and, by the look of them, they had no idea of moving. Indeed, upon closer inspection, I had doubts that they were the same people I had seen before, and began to wonder if the original tinkers had moved on and others taken their place. If that was the case there seemed little chance of the Home Farm ever becoming vacant and Meg and I and the children would have to winter in the gatehouse.

Sliding out from behind the sheltering bushes I walked home deep in thought until, remembering some wild strawberries that grew in the lane, I climbed the park wall and began to gather them for Mally's and Hal's tea. So intent was I that I didn't hear the approaching horseman until he reined in beside me and bade me 'goodmorrow'.

The voice was so familiar and yet so unexpected that I caught my breath and stayed my hand that was reaching for the small red fruits. Slowly I turned my head and, as I met the grey eyes examining me, knew that I grew pale and cold.

'I had not expected to find you here,' went on Captain Everton.

'And I had prayed never to see you again,' I said through dry lips and, feeling my legs tremble beneath me, abruptly sat down upon the bank behind me.

He swung out of the saddle, looping the reins over his arm as he regarded me steadily. 'Shall we walk to Summer Ho?' he asked. 'I presume you are living there?'

'In what's left of it,' I said bitterly. 'The gatehouse is a trifle cramped for two women and children but 'tis better than nothing.' Ignoring his hand, I scrambled to my feet hoping that my weak legs would carry me.

'May I walk with you?'

Speechless I gazed at him. 'No!' and even I

could hear the rousing hysteria in my voice.

'I have something to say to you.'

'You can have nothing that I wish to hear,' I broke in quickly. 'If you have any gallantry, any gentlemanly principles, I pray you go. I have no wish to be reminded that you have so far survived the war.' Blindly I turned and would have hurried away but he caught my arm and stayed me with a firm grip.

'In spite of your very natural sentiments, madam, I have much that must be said and must inflict my presence, however distasteful, upon you for a short while.'

Puzzled I stared at him and, even then, no presentiment of what was to come entered my mind.

'What mean you?' I asked, and made no movement to shake off his detaining hand.

'The open road is hardly the place for what I have to make known to you. Shall we walk on?'

I stood my ground. 'Sir, if you think one room shared with a maid and two children is the place for secret discussions you are sadly mistaken. You must either talk to me here or with others in earshot.'

He looked at me and I forced myself to meet his grey eyes, my gaze as cold and hard as his own. He hesitated then, after a while, shrugged slightly and said, 'So be it. There's a fallen tree yonder, shall we sit there?'

Disdaining his proffered arm, I led the way and seated myself with an assumption of the calm I was very far from feeling, while the Parliamentarian hitched his horse's reins over a branch and then stood looking down at me. Noticing the slight signs of ill-ease that he was at pains to conceal, I did nothing to help him, remaining silent until at last he spoke.

'What I have to say I fear will come as a shock.'

Again I waited in silence but now a fear was beginning to grow within me as I began to have an inkling of what Captain Everton would tell me.

'Maybe you've heard of the new rules of sequestration?' And then he said boldly, without trying to soften the blow or give me time to ready myself, 'Summer Ho has been sequestered to me.'

I sat in stunned silence, my breath caught in my throat and my heartbeats loud in my ears.

'Summer Ho is mine,' he repeated as though I had not heard.

'It belongs to me,' I insisted hoarsely.

He shook his head. 'No, by right of conquest it belongs to me.'

'No! Never! I will fight you for every stone you've left standing, for every blade of grass. 'Tis mine—my children's inheritance.' And even then I could not put into words the fact uppermost in my mind, that without Summer Ho we would starve.

Reaching to unhook his mount, he said without looking at me, 'I have nothing more to say, shall we go on?'

Jumping to my feet I seized his arm and shook it impatiently. 'But I have a great deal to say . . . So you Roundheads have turned thieves now, as well as murderers and destroyers. Is nothing too low for such as you? Afore God, I've never wished more that I was a man. An I carried a pistol I'd have as little compunction in shooting you as I would have in killing a fly.'

'You've already proved your murderous intentions, madam.'

He looked down at me, his face hard and his eyes as cold as ice. His fingers closed about my wrist, letting me feel his strength until my grip opened nervelessly. Releasing me with a contemptuous gesture he turned away while I looked at the angry white finger prints on my arm.

We walked in silence, he ahead of me, until we reached sight of Summer Ho and then I called,

'Let me go first—you'll afright the children.'

He looked at me and then down at his scarlet coat, knowing what I had in mind and I could see remembrance of that shameful day in his eyes as, without another word, I slipped past him and ran up the narrow stairs of the gatehouse. Meg had seen us coming and now started towards me with fearful apprehension, and the children catching fright from her set up a tearful wailing as I entered.

In spite of our fears, Captain Everton left

soon after inspecting the ruins of the house and making no attempt to see us again. Breaking the news to Meg and trying to stifle my own worry as I attempted to quiet her fears, I felt the hard knot of apprehension settle in my heart and wondered how we would manage now, for I had little doubt that Captain Everton would turn us out of the gatehouse. That we should starve was more than a probability, without a home it was a certainty, and at the thought I gathered the two babes into my arms and hugged them until they protested at the tightness of my grasp.

We were left with our fearful worries until early forenoon the next day when, hearing horsehoofs, I looked out of the narrow casement in time to see the Parliamentarian riding under the gatehouse. With fingers to our lips, Meg and I stilled the children's clamour and, eyes on each other, waited for what would happen. An imperative voice summoned me and, surrendering Mally to Meg's willing hands, I walked slowly downstairs and out into the sunlit courtyard.

'Have you somewhere we can talk?'

Wordlessly I led the way into the sunken garden and sat down on one of the stone seats there.

'I saw you inspecting the house,' I said without preamble. 'I expect that now you wish your soldiers had not been so thorough.'

He took a turn along the overgrown path for

142

a few paces and then returned, putting one booted foot upon the seat and leaning on his knee, regarded me gravely.

'I would have you know,' he said, 'that this sequestration order was none of my choosing.'

'And you accepted it,' I wondered, looking away.

'An I had not—others would!' he said sharply.

'And you felt you had a prior claim—after all you had burned it to the ground and had a hand in murdering its master,' said I bitterly.

In the sudden silence he slowly straightened, saying quietly, 'Remember, madam, if I had not brought him home he would have died on the battlefield.'

'Perhaps it would have been better if he had. You condemned him to worse than death. He was a man who had a *joie de vivre* and for the last months of his life he was useless, unable to leave his bed, with no use in his legs.' Looking up suddenly, I met the soldier's grey eyes and took a shuddering breath. 'You know he killed himself?'

'I'm sorry.'

'I don't want your sympathy,' I said bleakly, turning away.

'Then I'll not give it. If you must have someone to hate, my shoulders are broad enough to support it.'

The indifference of his tone stung me and I asked sharply 'Why have you brought me here? What would you have of me?'

143

Instead of answering, he abruptly asked a question of his own. 'You do not ask after the boy you shot?'

'I had supposed him recovered.' How could I tell him that I had been afraid to ask? Afraid of what I might hear.

'He will never regain the full use of his arm, though he has recovered in himself. He is my sister's boy and so I have an interest in him. Unless I have more children I intend to make him my heir.'

'To Summer Ho?' I asked painfully.

'No, I have other plans for that. To my estate at Mellish. I have hopes that he will marry my eldest daughter.'

'What do you want of me?' I asked again.

'I shall begin work on the house as soon as I may. Have you somewhere to go?'

My heart began to thump against my bodice. For some reason I had not been expecting the abrupt question, thinking in my own mind, with what I recognised as wishful thoughts, that we would not be turned out of our home.

'I ... hardly know,' I said at last, and then pride came to my rescue and I was able to strengthen my weak voice and say clearly, 'We will manage. An I was a man you would not find it so easy to take possession of Summer Ho but I suppose if I resist you will merely call up the aid of your soldiers.'

A slight flush showed in his lean cheeks as he

answered. 'As you have my actions already set in your mind, why should I give you the satisfaction of refuting them? Think of me what you will, and be out of here before the end of summer when I shall return with workmen to commence rebuilding.'

His voice that had grown warmer during our conversation was now hard and implacable again and I wondered briefly what he would have said if I had thrown ourselves on his kindness. A faint suspicion that he would not have been unkind passed my mind, but one fleeting glance up at his flinty grey eyes dispelled any such thoughts, and I hastily looked down at my hands clasped in my lap before he could read the despair in my own face.

'I had hoped,' he went on suddenly, 'that this meeting could be ended amicably, but I should have realised that a woman of your standing would prove too proud to hear reason or accept help from an enemy.'

'You have neither spoken reason nor offered help,' I pointed out indignantly, and had to stop and hide my face or he would have seen the tears that I struggled to suppress. 'But you are right,' I went on when I could speak safely, 'I would never accept help from such as you. You, Captain Everton, are and always will be my enemy.'

'I would be your friend!'

The words seemed to burst from him of their

145

own will and I stared at him in disbelief as I jumped to my feet.

'Never!' I cried, 'never! You have done me a great injury; there can never be anything but enmity between us.'

'So be it, madam,' he said bleakly, bowed curtly and walked quickly away without a backward glance, while my trembling knees gave way beneath me and I sank heavily back onto the seat, feeling that I had destroyed whatever sympathy he might have felt towards me, and half wishing that my anger had not betrayed me into such a foolish move when it would have been so much wiser to have played on his possible kindness. Rising to my feet, I hurried after him, and if I had found him would have humbled myself to him, but when I arrived in the courtyard he was already riding under the gatehouse and did not see me approaching.

My arm fell to my side and, feeling that the burden I carried was too much to be borne, I went into the gatehouse bracing myself to answer Meg's questions and still, for the time at least, the worst of her fears.

CHAPTER THIRTEEN

The summer lengthened into long hot days and all the while we washed and sewed and cooked and stored away, the problem of where we could go filled my mind to the exclusion of almost all else. My parents had died within a few days of each other of an infection caught at the beginning of the war and, owing to the difficulties of communication, they had already been dead for some weeks when I had news of their decease. Having waited for some time for a reply to my letter to Lettice, I at last heard that she and Denzil had fled to Holland and so two lines of possible help were gone. The last hope was that Ned Barlow could help in some way and, accordingly, one day in late August, I set off towards his house some four miles distant.

The walk was not unpleasant and, while longer than I would have cared for a while ago, the last months I had become used to hard work and seemed to have grown in strength.

Their house, like that of any prosperous yeoman, stood in the middle of the village street and, looking at the closed shutters and barred door, I knew that I would find little help there. I was just turning hopelessly away when a voice spoke at my ear and, turning, I saw an aged crone regarding me curiously.

'I wanted to speak with Master Barlow,' I answered her question. 'Do you know where I can find him?' She looked at me steadily for a moment or two and then, apparently making up her mind, smiled singularly sweetly.

'I'd say as you've come a tidy pace,' she said.

'Come you into my little cottage and take a drink of my elderberry wine.'

Following her into the dark interior of her home, I accepted a mug of sweet liquid and a seat beside the window, and soon my eyes grew accustomed to the dim light and I could distinguish the things about me. While everything was of the plainnest materials, all was clean and comfortable, the rag rug in front of the hearth was gay and cheerful, the earth floor newly sprinkled with water and swept. For a while I sat and sipped in silence and then the old dame, judging me refreshed enough for conversation, began to speak.

'Nurse I was to Master Ned, when he were a little lad. I'd just lost my own babe and was glad enough to cuddle another and forget the pain of my own.'

'Do you know where they are? Can I write to him?'

'In London somewhere, so he said, but I can't give you the direction. Don't think as how I even heard it.'

'Will he be away long?'

'That I can't say. Gone for the mistress's health. She ever was a poor scrap of a thing, not fit to be a wife, but he would have her. And much good it has done him. There's but the one boy and a string of graves in the Church. They've gone to seek a doctor's advice though I'd have thought all this gallivanting would have been more like to make her miscarry than staying at home.'

'So you've really no idea when they'll be back.' I sighed, suddenly feeling the effects of my walk and dreading the return journey.

She shook her head and began busying herself preparing the simple meal that she insisted I should take before setting out for Summer Ho. At first I protested, fearing to deplete her small larder but, after a while, understanding that I would hurt her more by refusal, I accepted her food and enjoyed the bread and cheese and beer she set before me.

'Who is managing the estate for him, has he no steward?' I asked as a forlorn hope at the door as I prepared to leave.

'The work is shared out between the near farms,' she explained. 'He's a good master and friend—all the neighbours are willing to help in his need.'

Thanking her for her hospitality, I set off homewards, sparing a thought for the man who had always been willing to help others and now was in need of help himself.

And of course, after that the days and weeks flew away while I sought for means of providing a home for my family, until at last I had to rest my wracked brains and admit that when Captain Everton arrived we would have to ask for his help and hope that he would not be unduly severe.

About the beginning of September, we were warned of the Roundheads' approach by the arrival of a waggon laden with tools and accompanied by three men and a boy. They accepted our presence with little apparent interest and seemed to have no idea of when to expect Captain Everton. With deceiving quiet, they set about their work and soon had some of the fine trees from the park cut down and seasoned while they looked to what could be saved of the burned building and what stone would have to be cut out and renewed.

Meg and I erected a barricade across the courtyard to keep the children away from the danger of falling masonry but soon Mally and little Hal were favourites with the men, and their hearts filled with joy as the men's clever fingers fashioned them new toys and playthings.

Some three weeks later, Captain Everton arrived, riding into the courtyard early one afternoon. Seeing him eye the children's barricade and glance up at our window, I knew that I had little need to make known our presence. However, I thought it would be better to go to him, rather than wait for him to seek me, and taking my courage in both hands, I ran down the stairs and into the yard, following him as he led his horse into one of the stables.

'Well?' he demanded as I stood in the doorway and my shadow crossed the floor to his feet. Without looking up from his task of unbuckling his saddle, he waited for my reply and I found it difficult to find words. Tossing the saddle over the top of a stall, he picked up a wisp of straw and began rubbing down the animal. 'What would you, ma'am?'

'We—I know you wanted us away from here,' I began, and even I heard how my nervousness made me sound haughty and arrogant.

'You hoped I'd change my mind?'

'No, indeed, I would not hang my children's fate upon so chancey a thing.'

'What then? Did you hope the King would win the final battle and that I'd be killed before now? Or did you suppose I'd suffer a change of heart and return Summer Ho to your keeping?'

'These thoughts had passed my mind,' I owned truthfully, and saw him blink at my candour, 'but I knew there was little likelihood of your Ironsides being beaten until we have reformed and recouped ... and I long ago decided that there was as much chance of your suffering a reverse of mind as there is of your falling in battle. Like your Ironsides, I begin to believe that you are invincible.'

Throwing aside the straw, he briefly caressed the horse's nose and came to lean in the doorway, folding his arms and looking down at me.

'It surprises me, then, to find you still here.'

''Tis not by my choice,' I burst out.

'This is not your way of fighting for Summer Ho?'

151

I looked at him blankly before shaking my head. 'No—think you I would willingly stay and see you tear down and alter all that I have loved? This was where I came as a bride, it was here that my children were born and here my husband died. If it were not for the babes, I'd rather by far be dead than see you destroy all my memories.'

'Memories are dull bedfellows,' he said strangely.

'I *treasure* them,' I answered proudly.

'So—you want to stay?'

'I have no choice,' said I bowing my head and unwilling to meet his eyes.

'Then *ask!*'

My eyes flew open and found his grey gaze full upon me. Looking at his cold eyes and hard face, an image of Harry as he had been when we were newly wed rose before my eyes, to be superceded by the flames that had consumed him as well as his house. 'No,' I whispered, backing away and shaking my head. 'No, I'll not ask you for anything, Master Roundhead.' Abruptly I turned and ran across the yard, dodging past the barricade and out into the Home Park.

The grass was cool and damp underfoot and a sweet breeze blew on my hot cheeks. I wandered under the tall trees until the shadows lengthened and the turmoil in my brain quietened. Soothed by the solitude, I turned for home, knowing what I must do.

I found Captain Everton seated with his men

in one of the empty stables. They had been talking together but stopped as I hesitated in the entrance.

'May I speak to you?' I called, and the soldier stood up and joined me. Taking my arm he led me away from the door and into the sunken garden.

It was not dark yet, the strange evening light robbing everything of its colour and clothing all in universal grey. Plucking a late rose from an overgrown bush, I inhaled its fragrance and then twirled its stem in my fingers, as I said, 'I must crave your pardon. I had meant to behave well—to ask you reasonably. Indeed I had my speech planned and I think that even you could not have resisted it, but all went wrong.'

'Did I speak my lines so ill?' he asked amused.

'Rather you spoke another part. One I'd not writ for you.'

'I believe 'tis ever so. In life I've found things never go as planned.'

Taking heart I looked up eagerly and drew a quick breath but, before I could speak, he suddenly said, 'The gatehouse will not be fit to live in this winter, you realise that? 'Tis scarcely more than a hovel.'

'Our ancestors lived in such places,' I made answer. 'An you will let us stay there I will make shift to do the same.' He looked down at me. 'Is there nowhere else?'

'There's a home farm but 'tis inhabited by

tinkers and while you might be able to remove them, I could not.'

'I'll go to see it in the morning,' he promised, but next day he returned from the farm with bad news.

The tinkers had left, leaving the farmhouse in ruins, it having shared the fate of Summer Ho, and only its stout walls remaining after a disastrous fire. And so it was settled, we would have to winter in the gatehouse.

CHAPTER FOURTEEN

As autumn came, so the work on Summer Ho proceeded. By October the new roof was on and the men could work inside sheltered from the wet and cold. That year winter came quickly. Early in November we had our first snowfall which soon turned to slush but thereafter the world was damp and bleak with a raw cold that seemed to eat into one's bones. We saw nothing of Captain Everton, he having returned to his home and children, but the workmen he left behind seemed aware of our plight and often we would find a gift of a snared rabbit or pigeon waiting on the doorstep in the morning. Even with these gifts our life was bitter and, after the discovery that most of our sheep was bad due to lack of salt, starvation was never far away. With lack of hay the cows' yield dropped and we had to keep the milk only for the children and cease making cheese and butter.

Soon Meg and I were forced to take it in turns to search the fields for whatever crops the farmer might have left in the ground, and this was precious little as the upheaval of the last few years had mightily upset the life of the country, the men who had gone for soldiers not having returned to till the land. However, by diligent searchings we usually found a few carrots or parsnips for the stewpot and even discovered in a far field a patch of those curious things called potatoes that Sir Walter Raleigh had brought back with him from his travels. These round vegetables seemed to have sown themselves from the ones left in the ground the previous year and, while neither so large or free from disease as those I had in London, proved a useful addition to our diet.

Seeking afield for sustenance brought another hardship; Letty's shoes were of use during the summer but with the damp and mud their silk and soft soles soon rotted and fell apart. Before long we were reduced to one pair of shoes between us, the ones Meg had been wearing the day Harry died. These were stout and strong and doubtless would last for many a month but, Meg, having larger feet than I, whenever I had to wear them I suffered agonies from their hard leather rubbing my smaller feet.

Even so we would have managed if the weather had not been against us but, by early winter, our stocks of wood and kindling were running out and we were forced to search even farther for the fuel for our fire. To conserve it we rose late and went to bed early and even so spent most of the day cold and miserable.

Meg and I took turn about, one seeking wood and food from the fields while the other stayed in the gatehouse minding the children and cooking what little food we had.

When I had waved to the children staring from the little lattice window a fitful sun had shone and, pulling my tattered cloak about me, I had quite enjoyed the walk to the fields. The nearby fields having long ago exhausted their supply, I was forced to seek farther away. Soon the short winter day was almost gone and I had found very few vegetables, only two soft carrots and a few small potatoes. The ground was hard and frozen, ice lay in the puddles and I was unable to move the earth to search under the top layer. As dusk fell I turned for home, clutching my spoils in my skirt, and just as I scrambled over the bank and back onto the road the first soft wet flakes of snow began to fall.

In my search I had wandered further than I had intended, the way was uphill and soon the cold and lack of food began to tell on my strength until, at last, I began to doubt whether I would ever manage the return journey. Bent against the wind, stumbling on frozen feet, I did not hear the horse until it was upon me. Suddenly it loomed up out of the grey swirling world, its shoulder struck me a glancing blow and I was flung headlong. Had not the rider cursed, halted his animal and returned, I verily believe I would have lain there until the snow covered me, so tired and weary was I.

But just as I was revelling in the sensation of cease from striving, the rider did return and rough hands pulled me to my feet, holding me upright when I would have fallen. I was shaken until my hood fell back from my hair, then urgent fingers brushed the wet snow from my face.

A man's voice exclaimed but, having just discovered the loss of my precious vegetables, I broke from his grasp and fell to my knees, scratching with desperate fingers among the light covering of snow.

Hands dragged at my shoulders but impatiently I shook them off, I found the carrots and clutched them to me but the tiny potatoes seemed lost forever and I was half sobbing with frustration as I was pulled ruthlessly to my feet.

'Leave them!' cried a voice in my ear, 'or we'll both freeze to death.'

'No, no, I must find them.' Desperately I fought the detaining grip and then quite suddenly my strength left me and I would have fallen but for the arms that closed around me. I felt myself lifted onto the horse's back, held there while the man mounted behind me and then strong arms encircled me as the reins were taken up.

Too weary to care, I lay in the circle of his arms and looked up at the face above me. A wide-brimmed hat shaded the man's face, snow half blinded me, but even in the growing dusk I had no doubt in whose arms I lay. A thick frieze cloak covered us both and, as the horse obediently started forward, I sighed, and for the first time in months let someone else bear responsibility.

'Oh, have you her safe, sir?' cried an anxious voice, and I wearily opened my eyes to find Meg's worried face peering up at me. 'I've been that afeared.'

'Have a care of my mount and I'll take your mistress inside.'

The next thing I knew was being set down on our rough bed and the cloak being peeled away from me, much as a person skins an orange. The neck of a flask was pressed to my lips and fiery brandy forced ruthlessly down my throat. My soaked shoes and stockings were pulled from my legs and my frozen feet chaffed and blown upon with warm breath. Then Meg appeared, stripped my clothes from me, rubbed warmth and life back into my cold limbs and tucked me into bed with hot bricks around me. Slowly warmth returned and, after a while, I was able to take in my surroundings.

158

In a corner Mally and Hal sat up in their cocoon of furs and blankets, their eyes huge and anxious in their pinched faces. I summoned a drowsy smile for their sakes before turning my head wearily towards the fire and the man sitting there.

Seeing I was awake, Captain Everton rose and, picking up a dish from the hearth, came to sit beside me. 'Drink this,' he commanded, spooning soup into my mouth.

Wondering at his ministrations, I obediently opened my mouth and found the soup surprisingly good.

'We'll talk in the morning,' he said firmly, presenting the spoon inexorably until the dish was empty. I saw him soothe the children before tucking the covers around them, then return to his seat by the fireplace. Several times during the night I awoke, my eyes irresistibly drawn towards the fire, and the still figure wrapped in a cloak, but when at last I awoke to find the thin light of day filtering into the tiny room he was gone and I wondered if I'd dreamed his presence.

But when Meg appeared, a thin powdering of snow gleaming on her cloak, and began to fry thick slices of bacon in a pan over the fire, I knew the fact of Captain Everton's arrival was real enough; not for months had we even smelled bacon. The children were out of bed eagerly clamouring for breakfast, when the Parliamentarian returned, but not until we had all eaten and Meg and the children had retired to the other end of the room did he move nearer me ready for the talk I knew we must have.

For a moment he stood looking down at me and I thought I read compassion in his eyes as he studied my face, which I knew had grown gaunt and pale.

'I must thank you for finding me last night,' I began bravely, 'an you had not, I think I must have perished.'

My voice faltered at the last word and suddenly he sat on the bed at my knees for which I was grateful. Captain Everton was too tall a man ever to make looking up at him a thing of pleasure.

'I am glad that I could be of service,' he said formally, the polite words meaningless and spoken automatically while his mind was elsewhere. Suddenly he drew breath and spoke with new determination as though having made up his mind. 'This cannot go on,' he said, 'you must realise that.'

'You mean we must leave here?' I asked slowly, each word an effort, the breath gasping in my throat. 'Truly, sir, we have nowhere else and if we leave here then my babes must die of cold and hunger. Surely you cannot...'

Hot tears rushed down my cheeks and, in my agitation, I gripped and twisted the blanket covering me.

'Nay, lass, nay.' Hands covered and held

160

mine. 'I had not meant that.' He waited until I grew calmer, then shook my hands to gain my attention. 'Had you really supposed I'd turn you and the children out into the snow?' he asked with a strange look.

I met his grey gaze fleetingly, then looked quickly away.

'I scarce know what to think,' I said, hanging my head, but had to add honestly, 'but I doubt me that you would really be cruel.'

A long sigh escaped him and he sat silent but still with my hands imprisoned in his. Presently he fell to playing with my heavy gold wedding band turning it round and round where it had grown loose on my thinning finger. Watching his bent head I grew curious at his hesitant manner and uncomfortable at the long silence. At last he looked up holding my eyes with his own.

'I ... have a proposition to put towards you,' he answered, his grip tightening on my hand until I could have cried out with pain. ''Tis obvious that you cannot stay here, you and the children are dying from the cold and lack of food. Summer Ho is almost finished now. Come the spring and the final touches will be made. I had ridden here with the intention of hiring servants and making all ready for my girls who will arrive before Christmas if the roads are passable—you, mistress, need a home and someone to provide for you and, to put it bluntly, I need a wife and mother for my daughters.'

Seeming to suddenly grow aware of his grasp on my hand, he relaxed his grip and rubbed my crushed fingers. At his words I made an involuntary gesture of withdrawal and he released me at once, studying my face intently.

'I cannot believe that ... you ask me to marry you?' I said slowly with a little gesture of repudiation. 'We—you and I—have nothing in common.'

'Only need.'

'And—that is enough?'

'Perhaps. Weddings are arranged. Mine was and I wager yours was too?'

'But then it was different—there were no differences between us. You and I—have much between us. The war—Harry. There is much that cannot be forgotten.'

'The English people will have to forget—and forgive—much in the next few years if there is to be peace again in our country. Remember Summer Ho belongs to me now, if you would have it for your son, you must marry me.'

I looked up. 'You'd leave it to him?' looking to Hal's golden head bent intently over some game.

'My daughters' portion is my former home, they are well provided for and need nothing else.'

'How do I know ...?'

'That I'd keep my word? The day we marry I'll make a will leaving it to the boy.'

A thousand thoughts whirled through my brain. Amazement, dismay and despair were foremost. Knowing I had no choice, yet I sought for means of escaping such a marriage and all it entailed. Captain Everton waited patiently yet inexorably for my reply, crushing my feeble resistance by his air of quiet strength.

'Well? he asked at last into the growing silence.

'I have no choice,' I said, my tone desolate.

'Do I offer so bad a thing?' he asked, a shade of amusement in his voice. 'Well, Anne, say me yea or nay.'

I could find no words, my lips dry and trembling. After a while I put out my hand blindly and found it at once taken in a warm grip.

'I'll make arrangements,' said Captain Everton, and stood up as though about to begin that minute. From his height he looked down at me, a smile touching his lips. 'Don't look so frightened,' he advised quite gently. 'You'll find I'm no ogre.'

With these words he turned and strode out of the room leaving me limp and exhausted against the pillow. Under cover of the blankets I squeezed my hands together, my fingers twisting in agitation as fears and fright welled up in me. What did the future hold I wondered despairingly.

CHAPTER FIFTEEN

For the first time since that holocaust in March the tall chimneys of Summer Ho belched forth smoke as huge fires were lit to dry out the rebuilt house. I never ventured there but Meg did, returning wide-eyed and agog with the innovations Captain Everton had instituted.

' 'Tis nothing like it was,' she reported. 'The rooms be set out all altogether different. There's no Great Hall for one thing but the pannelling's a marvel And the kitchens...' She flung up her hands as words failed her. 'Well, it'll be a joy to be a kitchen maid there, I can tell you.'

Luckily the icy weather held and the heavy waggons, loaded with furniture and bedding, managed the journey from Alton with ease. The sounds of their wheels brought Hal and Mally to the doorway with me after them, to grip their leading strings and hold them out of harm.

Seeing us, Captain Everton crossed the yard. 'Come and see the new fittings,' he said, swinging Hal to his shoulder and taking Mally's hand. He looked back, raising his eyebrows imperiously as I hesitated. 'Come!' he urged in a manner little short of a command. ' 'Twill be your home, you have a right to set things in the place you desire.'

Still hesitating, I bit my lip and looked away. Not since it had been burned down had I set foot in Summer Ho, and the thought of returning to my former home filled me with memories and disquiet. As though sensing my unease, the soldier suddenly called to Meg and, setting down the children, sent them to her. His hand took mine and tucked it into the crook of his elbow, holding it firmly there as he drew me away from the doorstep and across the yard.

At the flight of steps that led up to the front door he released me, letting me enter the house alone. To my relief there was nothing of the old Summer Ho remaining. I might have been in any new house; the smell of new wood and plaster hung in the air and the noise of an army of helpers filled the interior as furniture was carried to the rooms, curtains and tapestries hung.

'I've engaged some servants,' said Captain Everton, 'but of course you will be at liberty to make what changes you wish.'

Nodding, I moved away, turning to look about me. As Meg had said, the Great Hall had gone and in its place was a modern entrance hall, much smaller than the original, with an elegant dogleg staircase leading to the upper floors and several doors leading out of it.

Captain Everton went with me on my exploration, saying little but ready to offer companionship when I had need of it. At last I had seen over the whole house and we had returned to what would be the parlour. Leaning against the wide windowseat, I looked out at the familiar scene, the new panes of glass cold against my cheek. Behind me the fire crackled and a floorboard creaked as the soldier moved his weight from one foot to the other in front of the fireplace.

'My girls arrive before Christmas,' he said abruptly, 'and I think it best that we be married before then.'

'Do they know about me?' I asked.

'Yes—I've explained the situation to them.'

'Will they accept me—as a mother I mean?' I turned to face him across the darkening room.

'I hope so—Bess might be difficult, but Jennet has a loving heart. She will love anyone who will let her.' His lips curved in sweet reminiscence and I suddenly realised that his daughters meant as much to this man as Mally and little Hal did to me.

'I'll do my best for them,' I assured him with a rush of feeling and shivered, suddenly aware that the house was not warm yet.

'Come to the fire,' he urged and placed a chair for me. He kicked the logs into flame, with one black-booted foot, and then stood looking down at me, one arm stretched along the carved mantlepiece. I fell to pleating the material of my skirt, dropping my head so as not to meet his steady grey gaze. At last he moved to cover my nervous fingers with his hand and, startled, I looked up to find his

166

expression kind and compassionate.

'You and the children must move in here,' he said. 'All is ready and 'tis pointless for you to make shift in the gatehouse any longer.'

'But you—' I began, and broke off in confusion.

'This house is big enough for both of us— and to still any gossiping tongues, you and I will ride into Alton tomorrow to be wed.'

My fingers twisted in his grasp. 'So soon?'

He held my fluttering hands firmly and bent over me. 'Tomorrow,' he repeated. 'There's no need for delay and you have not altered your mind?'

There was a question in his voice and, resolutely turning my mind from thoughts of what might have been, I shook my head while visions of a dark, scarred face danced behind my closed eyes.

'I'll not jilt you,' I said with an attempt at lightness.

He sighed with an emotion I could not name and then said, 'While we're away Meg can move the children into the house. I think it best that we have a few days to ourselves, among strangers, and have sent a servant to bespeak us rooms in The White Horse at Alton. You will be able to visit the market and buy anything you need'.

'You are kind,' I said, and stood up shaking out my old worn skirts. 'I must make arrangements, if you'll excuse me.'

Taking my hand, he carried it to his lips and held it so long that perforce I raised my eyes to his face. An unexpected thrill of shock ran through me as our eyes met, then I dragged my hand from his grasp and fled the room, his laughing 'Goodnight' echoing in my ears.

Sleep was long coming to me that night. Thoughts of Ashley flitted through my head and his words of long ago rang in my mind. Circumstances change he had said, speaking the truth where I was concerned. Had I really half thought that he would hear of my circumstances and come to rescue me. Such things only happened on the stage I told myself and yet, I was strangely reluctant to give up my single state again ... and what exactly had I seen in those grey eyes as Captain Everton kissed my hand? Certainly not the cold indifference of a marriage of convenience— and yet what else could there be between such differing persons? Like to like, my father always said and what could be more opposed than a Royalist lady and a soldier in the New Model Army?

These questions still filled my mind the next morning and I rode quietly into Alton, now and then stealing glances at the man in front of me. Having only the one horse, I had to ride pillion, one hand tucked into Captain Everton's belt and the view quite obscured by his broad shouders.

We found our room and private parlour

awaiting us at the Inn and here Captain Everton left me while he went to make sure that arrangements for our wedding had been made. We were to be married in St Lawrence's Church, where Colonel Bolles had so valiantly lost his life when surprised by Roundheads from Farnham.

Very soon James Everton was back, bringing with him the landlady bearing a bowl of mulled wine.

'I thought you'd like to visit the market,' he said, when our glasses were filled and she had left.

'I would, but...'

Understanding my hesitation, he slipped a little silk purse into my lap, and smiled at me as I looked up in query. 'Now, Anne, pray accept a little gift from me. After all we are to be wed this afternoon. Swallow your pride for once.'

Fingering the smooth silk, I looked away. ''Tis not that...' I began, and paused, at a loss to explain my feelings.

'Cannot you forget that by force of circumstances we are enemies...?'

''Tis not by circumstances alone. You are a Parliamentarian by force of your convictions, you can't wear that uniform and say otherwise, while I...' He did not speak but I knew his penetrating grey gaze was upon me, and went on bravely. 'While I... have my own thoughts and feelings on these matters.'

'It would be very strange had you not.'

His voice was calm and, taking courage, I turned my head to meet his eyes and went on. 'You must realise—I must tell you—that even though I have married you, my convictions will remain unchanged.'

'Are you telling me that you will act as a spy or poison the Protector in his sleep if he should visit us?'

His voice was amused and I knew a flush covering my cheeks.

'You—should not laugh...' I rejoined coldly, gathering the pitiful remnants of pride around me.

'Anne—I had but meant to tease. Since that night I found you in the snow you have been a poor quiet thing. I have not seen you laugh or smile at the children—or even flash your temper at me.'

'How could I do so—when you are my benefactor?'

There was a silence in the little room, and then Captain Everton spoke quietly. 'Is that how you think of me—as your benefactor? I had hoped for something—warmer.'

I twisted the strings of the purse about my fingers. 'I thought our marriage was one of convenience.' My voice was so low that I could not be sure that the man opposite had heard me. Suddenly he moved and sat down beside me on the settle. His hand covered my restless fingers and firmly removed the purse from my grasp, then he took both my hands in his,

170

holding them until I looked up and met his eyes.

'It could be more than that.'

'How so?' I faltered, and hung on his words, yet not knowing what I wanted him to answer.

'Our meetings have been scarcely auspicious—and yet I feel that under other circumstances, had the occasions been different, we could have been—friends.'

Dazed I stared at him. The coincidence of his choice of words making my head reel. 'Perhaps,' I managed to say.

'I know that you are not indifferent to me.' He smiled at the word. 'You have told me often enough that you hated me.'

The tone of his voice made me glance up and something in his expression made me cry out truthfully. 'No—I was wrong. I don't—have never, hated you. It was the war, all that you stood for that I hated.'

'We have that to build on,' he said quietly, his grip tightening around my fingers. 'For you must know that my feelings for you have been far from indifferent for some time.'

I looked at him blankly, my bewilderment in my face. 'Then you have a vastly odd way of showing it,' I burst out rudely.

'I'll endeavour to do better in the future,' he told me gravely, and I grew suddenly quiet at his words.

CHAPTER SIXTEEN

Snow was powdering the road as we travelled back to Summer Ho and I was glad to tuck my head into my husband's broad back and cling to his stout belt as the horse trotted smartly over the frozen ground. Fine snow found its stinging way up my nose and made me sneeze.

'Cold, Anne?' enquired my husband turning his head to look at me. 'We'll soon be there.'

The wide-brimmed hat shadowed his face but, even so, I could see his eyes and the expression in their depths made me catch my breath. Concern, tenderness and something more showed in their grey tones and, impulsively, I unhooked my fingers from his belt and slid my arms around his waist. For a moment longer he looked at me and then turned to face the road, but now one of his hands covered mine and we journeyed home in this fashion.

Meg had the door open as we rode under the gatehouse and I could see her anxious figure standing on the steps in the cold winter twilight as James Everton lifted me down from the pillion seat. Two small figures clung to her skirts and I ran up the stairs to gather Mally and Hal into my arms.

'Here's your Mama back!' I cried kissing their silky heads, 'and there's a surprise for you

172

in my bag.'

At once they were clamouring for their presents and the uneasy moment and meeting was over. The door closed behind me and I looked over my shoulder to see Captain Everton standing there regarding us with something like hunger in his eyes and I pushed the children forward.

'Make your bows to Captain Everton,' I told them.

Above their heads his eyes sought mine. 'Methinks they are young enough to accept calling me father,' he said quickly before bending from his tall height to accept their salutes.

I had thought that in the confusion of the moment he had not noticed that I had not answered him but, after Meg had taken the children and we were sitting over our dinner, he said, 'I feel that children need a stable secure home—one that contains both mother and father. It may be painful to you, Anne, but for the children's sake I feel that they should call me father.'

I toyed with a spoon and the golden foam of a syllabub. 'And your daughters? Will they call me mother?' I asked.

'They are older. Their mother is still very dear to them, but I feel that Jennet will copy your own children.'

'And Elizabeth?'

'She is eleven, almost an adult. She and her

173

mother were very close. Since Mary died, Bess has become a very quiet, withdrawn child—I fear we may have difficulty with her.'

And I knew he was right as soon as I saw her. They arrived a few days before Christmas and I first saw her standing on the doorstep, a small upright figure, her hood falling back to show her smooth red-gold hair. Adult and self-possessed, her cool grey eyes examined me coldly above her younger sister's head, and I felt as though a shaft of ice had been set in my heart. Then Jennet ran forward to take my hands.

'Are you my new Mama?' she cried, and I looked down eager to accept her overture. The face that looked up at me could not have been more different to her sister's. Rosy cheeks and bright brown eyes were framed in a knot of warm brown curls, and I knew at once that I would love her. Drawing her to me, I found her body none so different to Mally's. Warm and soft, she still retained the feel of babyhood, but when Elizabeth dutifully accepted my embrace I might have held a board of wood.

I saw a glance pass between father and daughter before I turned away to bring forward Mally and Hal to be introduced. Soon Jennet's cloak was tossed aside and she was joining happily in the younger children's games, but Elizabeth stayed aloof, her hands clasped in front of her as she walked about the room.

Captain Everton was called away on business and she scarcely waited until the door was closed behind him before showing her true feelings.

'These pictures are very fine!' came her high young voice across the room. 'I imagine my father bought them—weren't all your things lost in the fire?'

'You know they were,' I answered calmly.

'But they must have been of your husband's family. Wasn't your father a merchant?'

'Artists don't refuse to paint business men you know. Their money is quite as good as an aristocrat's.'

'If not their antecedents,' she smiled thinly. 'Ours go back to the Norman Conquest.'

'Then 'tis time your thin noble blood was thickened with some good bourgeois,' I answered firmly refusing to let her annoy me but, all the same, I knew we would not be friends when, later that evening, we stood on the landing while I showed the two girls their room and explained the layout of the house.

'The nursery is here,' I said, pointing to where Mally and Hal were sleeping. 'And your room is next door. Perhaps when you are older you'd like your own rooms but I thought that for now you'd like to be together.'

'Where does my father sleep?' asked the older girl looking about.

'Here,' and I indicated a door at the end of the corridor.

'And you?' Above the candlelight her eyes were very wide and pale.

'With him,' I answered quietly.

'My mother always had her own chamber. 'Tis vastly more elegant so.'

'But not nearly so comfortable!'

For a moment our eyes met as she stared at me with undisguised hostility, then snatching up her sister's hand she whisked into her bedchamber and closed the door smartly. Sighing, I went downstairs to a little back parlour that I had made my own, where I could sew and read or be alone and think. And there James Everton found me when he came in search of me some time later.

Without a word he removed the embroidery from my lap and possessed himself of both my hands, drawing me up to stand within the circle of his arms. Sighing I leaned my aching head against his chest.

'Troubled, my love?' he asked into my hair.

'It will not be easy,' I answered, wondering at my own feelings as he held me. Not so long ago I would have thought mad anyone who suggested marriage between a Roundhead and myself and yet here I was married to the man who had burned Summer Ho and been enemy to me and my kindred. For months I had told myself that I hated him and yet I had found that was not true. On our wedding night I found that his touch had not filled me with distaste and now his arms were a haven of security and comfort. Emotions seemed to rear within me and I was confused and uncertain of my feeling. Honour and Royalist dogma told me that I should hate and despise this man—and, fight against it how I would, I knew I had kinder feelings for him, While unable to hate the soldier, my heart refused to betray Ashley Death.

'The bales of cloth have arrived,' he said, seeming to sense my disquiet and setting me free. 'You and the girls must choose your material and mayhap you could make new gowns for Christmas.'

'I fear it would be a great rush.'

'There are wenches to help now. Folk have been applying at the back door for days—the war is over and they have need of work.'

'I'll see what we can do,' I promised.

The next morning we opened the bales, unstitching the heavy linen that covered the rolled material and setting it aside for dish clouts and cloths. Not for years had I seen such colours and materials, and Meg and I exclaimed our delight. With what I thought was great nobility, I offered Elizabeth the length of olive green velvet, though I coveted it for myself.

''Tis just the colour for your hair and complexion,' I assured her, thinking to please.

'My mother always put me in blue,' she sniffed.

'The only blue is a length for the new

servants' livery. Surely you don't want that?' I asked sharply.

She settled at last for a dark brown that made her hair appear golden and seemed well pleased with her choice. While Jennet chose a rose-coloured wool for her and Mally, I presented my dear Meg with a red linsey-woolsey and soon all was industry.

Elizabeth proved herself a good seamstress and, while Meg cut out, she and I sewed seams and darts and gathers until out fingers were sore, but the prospect of new clothes made our needles fly and the day before Christmas all was finished and we could rest from our labours.

The kitchens were filled with warmth from the huge ovens and delightful smells from the food cooling there. Meg and I could hardly believe that a few weeks ago we were destitute and almost on the point of starvation. We were a little unsure how to behave for we had heard tales that the Parliamentarians did not keep Christmas but when, on Christmas Eve, we began to sing the old carols with the children, a man's voice joined in and we knew that we had done right.

The nearby Church was closed and the parson long gone so we knew there was no chance of a service, and we had to be content with reading from the bible among ourselves. In the afternoon we handed round our presents in remembrance of the gifts the Magi had

178

brought that first Christmastide.

James had fashioned two wooden hobby horses for Hal and Mally, while I had made them two rag babies, for little children dearly love a soft bundle to carry around with them. For the older girls I'd bought lengths of ribbons. Jennet flung her arms round me and shyly presented me with a needlecase she had worked, but Elizabeth set hers aside with little sign of interest and said nothing.

James gave the girls a heavy silver chain but I was surprised when he dropped a little leather box into my lap. For a moment I looked at it, lying on my embroidery, then picked it up with hands that trembled a little.

'I had not thought . . .' I began, stealing him a glance, and then broke off for I had managed to open the box and there, on its bed of red velvet, was a chain with a pear-shaped pearl pendant. 'It's—beautiful,' I whispered, touching it with one delicate finger.

Hands took the chain from its soft bed and slipped it over my head. James's fingers brushed my neck and then the pendant lay cold on my bosom.

'I have something for you,' I said shyly, reaching among the folds of my skirt for the pocket that dangled from its ribbon, 'but knew not when to give it you.'

I held the folded handkerchief out to him and watched anxiously as he examined it. The black and white needlework pattern seemed right for one of his convictions but would the lace, that I had been unable to resist sewing round the hem, be too rich for his tastes?

Looking up, he smiled, and I knew all was well. 'I am touched,' he said softly, 'that among all your preparations you had time to sew for me.'

The children were busy in front of the fire, and we might have been alone in our shadowy corner of the room. Sitting beside me, Captain Everton possessed himself of my hand and carried it to his lips. The flickering light from the fire played across his face and, across the shadows, our eyes met and held.

'All goes well, my wife?' he asked meaningly.

'I pray so,' I answered breathlessly, as he bent his head and kissed my finger tips one by one.

CHAPTER SEVENTEEN

The world was held in the grip of winter for weeks after Christmas. The New Year brought gales and blizzards which froze the ponds and covered dirty snow with fresh pristine whiteness. Birds came to the door for food and were frozen fast overnight to the branches where they had roosted. Milk left in the dairy became solid in the buckets and our fingers grew red and cracked. It seemed that we would never become warm again and we lived by the fires, scarce moving save to go to our beds.

At last one day dawned that seemed warmer than the others; for a few hours after the midday meal a faint heatless sun shone and, bundling the children into thick cloaks and scarves, I hurried them out into the white landscape that surrounded Summer Ho.

Bare trees were silhouetted blackly against the pale sky, while now and then branches cracked sharply and fell to the ground under the weight of snow and ice. Everything seemed different under the anonymity of the snow covering it, and the children ran around shrieking with excitement after their enforced inactivity, sweeping walls bare with their hands, tasting cold snow on their tongues and discovering the joy of a snow fight.

We had wandered into the sunken garden when I caught my breath in surprise and was glad that the children were a few paces behind me and intent upon their games. Breaking the clean snow in front of me was a line of footprints. Following them with my eye I saw that they led to the old stone summer house set back in the far wall. I should have retraced my steps and called for help, but some instinct made me turn to the children and send them back to the house while I went on alone.

At first I thought I had been mistaken and the summer-house was empty, then a movement within made me start back with an exclamation but, before I could take to my heels, a hand came out and caught my wrist in a strong grasp. I grew quiet then, looking at the embroidered glove and lace cuff that covered the hand that held me.

'Anne, Anne,' said a deep voice and I was pulled close against a man's chest, icy cold lips found mine and our breaths mingled as mouths grew warm.

'Ashley, oh, Ashley,' I could only murmur, while my heart cried out to know why he had not come sooner.

His soft leather gloves were tossed aside and his hands touched my face and hair as he pushed back my hood. His touch was hard and quick, almost as if he could not believe I was real. Black eyes blazed into mine and I hung in his arms breathless, then, with a half-smothered cry, he gathered me back into his arms, rocking me against him. For a long time I surrendered, giving myself up to the bliss of his passion, only grateful that he returned the emotion that I had suppressed for so long.

At last I became aware of the growing dusk and, recalled to my surroundings, slid a hand between our mouths.

'I must go!' I cried dismayed, 'if they should find you here...'

'Stay—no-one will miss you.'

'The children—I see them into bed. And it must be almost dinner time...'

'Leave them,' he urged and, against my will,

I shook my head. 'Then, come again, or let me in.'

My heart raced. ''Twould be too dangerous.' I raised my hand again as he would have protested and touched his lips tightly with my fingers. 'I'll come—later when 'tis safe.'

He gently bit my detaining finger. 'I have your word?'

'My promise.' Looking up at his dark face, I saw his teeth gleam in the soft half light, his long black hair moving slightly in the cold wind.

Behind him something moved and, feeling me stiffen, he quickly released me and turned, one hand on his sword hilt. In that second he changed from a lover to a fighting man, his weight lightly balanced on the balls of his feet, every muscle tensed and ready for action.

''Tis nothing,' I assured him. 'Some animal perhaps.'

Black eyes glanced down at me and, for a moment, I had the curious impression that he did not see me, then he perceptibly relaxed, loosening his grip on the sword and whistling between his closed teeth.

'I am—on business' he explained softly, while his eyes searched the dim garden. 'No one must know I am here.'

'No-one shall,' I promised and touched his hand, before picking up my skirts, I ran back to the house.

No-one seemed to have missed me and,

except for Elizabeth who glanced up as I entered, none seemed interested in my activties. Dinner seemed to take an age that night, while every nerve strained with impatience. At last the boards were uncovered and I excused myself on pretext of a headache.

'Don't go!'

James Everton's words stopped me at the door and I slowly turned back into the room, my mouth dry with sudden fright. His grey eyes were very clear and bright as he regarded me from the other side of the table.

'What—do you mean?' I managed to ask at last.

'Take some wine with me. It will do your head good.'

Without waiting for me to answer, he lifted the decanter and, pouring wine into two long-stemmed glasses, carried them to the settle by the fire and, perforce, I had to join him.

Taking an unwary sip at the drink, it caught my throat and I choked over its sweetness, spilling some wine on my dress before I could control my hand.

Without a word, my husband mopped my skirt, while I tried to draw breath and still my smarting eyes.

'Something bothers you?' he asked, when I'd regained some measure of control.

'No—of course not,' I answered sharply.

'It seems to me that you have something on your mind.' Taking my hand in his he fell to playing with my fingers, a thing which until now I had rather liked but, irritated, I snatched my hand away.

'I pray you, sir, let me be,' I cried pettishly and, to my surprise, fell to crying. Blinking away the tears, I turned my head aside, pride making me hope that the man beside me would not see.

Fingers pinched my chin and my face was turned towards him. For a moment grey eyes stared into mine and I had a longing to tell him all that had happened in the garden, before thoughts of what would happen to Ashley, should I betray him, filled my mind and I closed my mouth on the breath I had taken.

The glass was removed from my hand and my head tipped ruthlessly up. His kiss was like none I had received from him before and, coming so close on Ashley's, left me confused and gasping. Bewildered and half afraid of my entangled feelings, I pushed him away and, the minute my hands touched his cheek, his grip loosened and I was free. A moment longer he held my hand.

'Stay with me, Anne,' he said softly and momentarily I thought to hear a note almost of entreaty in his voice, 'or does your head still pain you?'

Standing up, I dragged my hand free. 'My head—I must go to my room,' I gasped incoherently and then almost ran from the room.

Waiting only to make sure that the soldier had not followed me, I pulled a cloak about my shoulders and, running down a back staircase, let myself out into the icy night.

Frost had made the soft snow crisp and it crunched beneath my feet, each step sending an icy shower to fill my shoes. The moon had risen and hung, golden and cold, in a sky that seemed filled with stars. As though trying to leave my doubts behind me, I ran to the little stone house, sliding and slipping in my haste.

Ashley's arms were as warm and strong as I remembered them and, for a while I was content to lie against his chest my cheek against the steady beat of his heart.

'I understand you are married?' he said at last.

I lifted my head. 'What else could I do? We were destitute and the children starving—I waited, truly I did—I hoped you'd come.'

His arms tightened. 'I didn't know.'

'I thought Letty might have told you.'

'Lettice?' he seemed amused. 'Why should she? We don't correspond.'

'Oh.' I digested this in silence, then felt compelled to ask. 'You know about the baby?'

'Yes.' His answer was uncompromising and I knew I must not ask any more questions. Indeed, he seemed to feel that the time for conversation was over and action must now be taken, for he changed his hold and, sliding an arm around my waist, urged me along the walk.

'We mustn't linger here,' he said. 'We have far to go.' In astonishment I turned to look up at him. 'What do you mean?' I gasped.

At once he stopped, his arm leaving my waist.

'I—had supposed that you intend to leave with me.'

'Leave! But Ashley, what of the children? What of Mally and Hal?'

He looked down at me, his face inscrutable. 'Surely Meg will care for them.'

Speechless, I stared at the snow at my feet, while the cold seemed to creep into my body, until I folded my arms and hugged myself to keep from shaking with the chill that filled me.

'Come girl,' whispered a voice, soft and persuasive in my ear. 'I've never been one for dalliance on a cold bed, let's away to find a warm inn ... and then in the morning if you've still a mind to, you can return to your Roundhead an you must.'

Involuntarily, I stepped back but, at that moment, footsteps crunched on the snow behind us and, with sudden dread, I knew who was there.

'I pray you, sir, unhand my wife!' said Captain Everton, and never have I heard a voice so cold and deadly, so devoid of human feelings.

'No—'tis not as it seems,' I cried starting towards him, but he scarcely glanced in my direction, all his attention being focused on the man before him.

'Will you give me satisfaction?' he demanded.

Ashley laughed, and swept his hat from his head to the ground, where it lay like a dead crow. 'An your wife has, *you* needs must,' he said, and I quailed at his words.

Steel rasped as swords were drawn and then rang and clashed in the first flurry as both men attacked. Numbly I watched as they leaped and lunged, black and indiscriminate against the snow like puppets at a fair. Soon the whiteness was churned beneath their heavy boots, and white puffs of breath at their mouths told of their exertions.

'Stop—oh, stop!' I wailed and knew that neither heard me. I was the cause of their contention and neither was aware of me.

And then, quite suddenly, the fight was ended. Ashley leaping back to avoid a lunge by the other man, slipped and fell, to lie breathing heavily as he looked up at his adversary.

The Parliamentarian drew back his sword and only then did I break the spell that held me and dashed forward.

'James, no!' I ran to his side, ready to hang onto his sword arm but, as I reached him, I knew that it would not be necessary; already at the sound of my voice, the sword point had wavered and dropped. Relief and thankfulness washed over me and I sucked in a breath of icy air. Although to me, Ashley's fall and my husband's action seemed to have taken ages, in actual fact very few seconds had passed since I saw the Cavalier slip and now, in a blurr of movement at our feet, he was upright and I saw steel flash wickedly as he lunged at the man beside me. Whether he realised that Captain Everton had just spared his life, I had no idea as, with an inarticulate cry, I flung myself forward and caught the sword among the enveloping folds of my cloak.

The weapon was jerked out of his hands and the two men stood on the path warily eyeing each other. Apart from their harsh breathing, the silence grew until an owl's melancholy cry recalled us all to our surroundings and slowly James turned to look at me.

'I believe 'tis your choice,' he said coldly.

Clasping my hands together, I looked about at the gaunt, lifeless trees, at the ruined snow at our feet and the bright stars above; last of all, and that most reluctantly, at the men waiting for my reply. Never before had I seen men so plainly contrasted. Ashley tall and elegant, lace dripping from his wrists and at his boot tops, his long black hair gleaming in the moonlight, and James Everton immaculate in the uniform of the New Model Army, his orange sash worn proudly over one shoulder. Opening my mouth, I tried to speak, but no sound came from my parched lips. At last, unable to find my voice, I crossed to the soldier and slowly touched his arm.

Unresponsive to my hand, he looked grimly at the other. 'You'd best go,' he said harshly.

And while I kept my eyes lowered, I heard Ashley pick up his sword, return it to its sheath and then, with a curious sound, half laugh half sob, he turned and walked away.

Without a word, my husband gripped my arm above the elbow and led me towards the house. All at once my legs began to tremble and seem made of lead. With quick beating heart I stumbled on, while he seemed not to notice my distress until, suddenly, the sky and stars and black chimneys of Summer Ho began a mad dance around my head—a gaping pit seemed to open at my feet and I plunged into a spinning void.

CHAPTER EIGHTEEN

When I opened my eyes it was morning and the winter sun streamed in at the windows. I lay still and tense while memories of the events of the night before filled my mind, then knowing that, however much I desired to stay in bed and escape the consequences of my own actions, I must face the future some time, I rang the bell for Meg.

My husband was in the library and I paused outside the room, my heart beginning to hammer against my ribs while I summoned up the courage I needed, before scratching at the door, I entered quickly before my resolution should fail me. He looked up at my entrance and I saw an expression of surprise fleet over his face.

'I had not expected to see you,' he said, and I saw that he was wearing boots and that his cloak lay over a chair.

'You are going somewhere?' I asked sharply, failing to keep the anxiety out of my voice.

For a moment his hands were still among the papers he was folding. Silence grew between us as he tucked the packet into his coat before replying. Buttoning the cloth across his chest, he said baldly,

'I go to London...'

As though fascinated, I watched his lean brown fingers busy with the red material. He settled the heavy buff coat about his shoulders and at last, as he arranged the folds of the bright orange sash, I found my voice.

'You go to inform about Ashley?'

'I have been recalled to London by General Cromwell.'

Still I could not let matters be and went across the room to him, to ask pleadingly, 'You will not seek him?'

Grey eyes looked at me bleakly. 'Madam your paramour is safe from me, whether he is as safe from Cromwell's spytakers 'tis another matter.' Tucking his gauntleted gloves into his

191

belt, he swung the cloak over his shoulders and looked down at me impatiently. 'An you have nothing more to say, I will take my leave.'

'James!' I held out my hands to him. 'Must you go like this—cannot we part friends?'

He stiffened. 'Friends, madam? Friends have trust between them.'

He made no move to take my hands and I let them fall to my sides, turning my head away to hide my face from him.

'You must believe...' I said painfully, 'that he is not ... has never been ... my lover.' How could I tell the implacable man before me that at last I had seen Ashley Death for what he was? Gay and brave, but at heart cold and spoiled, ever ready to accept but not prepared to ever give anything of himself in return. Last night my husband had seemed ready to love me but now, when I needed him and realised that all these months I had returned that emotion unknowingly, he was cold and distant, believing me false.

'Have I your permission?' he asked tiredly, and I knew that I could not keep him longer.

Turning to look at him, I saw that he had put on his broad-brimmed hat and that its shadow shielded his face from my eyes. Pride came to my rescue and I lifted my chin to say, with a voice that only shook a little, 'Pray you be careful, the roads will be scarcely passable.'

'Your concern does you credit,' he said mockingly. 'As you have said before, I am invincible.'

I hung my head, recalling how I had said I hated him and wished him dead. When I looked up he had gone, the door hanging open and the room strangely empty.

With his departure the snow and cold weather went too, soon the world was adrip and then shoots and green things began to appear in the damp earth—and with their coming sickness came too. Some sort of fever appeared in the village and I forbade the children to leave the house and courtyard. Had I been less preoccupied with myself and my own unhappiness, I might have realised that such orders would only antagonise Elizabeth, but not until I found the two older girls slipping under the gatehouse from the road did I suspect that I had been disobeyed.

'What do you?' I asked sternly and at once the smile left Jennet's plump cheeks. 'You know I have said you must not go to the village.'

''Tis father's birthday,' she burst out, while the older girl said nothing, 'and we did but go to the pedlar to buy a present.'

'Did you speak to or touch anyone?' I asked quickly. and knew a presentiment of fear as they glanced at each other.

'Only a little boy—he was sitting on a doorstep and wanted a drink.'

At that moment Meg ran up, horror on her face and in her voice. 'Oh, miss,' she cried and I think I knew what she would say even before she drew breath. 'They do say there's pox in the village.'

'Dear God!' I whispered, gazing at the girls, while the fearful spectre of death seemed to dance before me.

'What'll we do, miss, what'll we do?' asked Meg, her voice rising with panic.

Quite suddenly I was icy calm and knew what I must do. As a child I had taken the cowpox from a milkmaid and, knowing that it was said to be efficacious against the effects of smallpox, decided that I should be the one to nurse the girls. A room was prepared for us, well away from the rest of the house inhabitants, with truckle beds and cooking utensils. Once inside, a blanket soaked in vinegar was hung at the door sealing us in, and we waited to see what was in store for us.

Days passed—a week—and we dared to hope. A letter arrived from James saying that the Parliament had word that the King was contemplating seizing a port in Kent for access to the continent, but such news seemed to have little import for us and I put the letter aside. That night Jennet was restless and, by morning, I knew my worst fears were realised. I wished I had separated the sisters for then, Elizabeth, who showed no signs of illness, would have been safe. I did the best I could, sending her to the little inner dressing room, hoping she would be away from harm there, for none know how it is caught; some say it's born on the air and others that a touch, or the clothing of a victim may contaminate another.

On the evening of the third day, Jennet was burning with fever. I clipped her bright hair close against her head and was bathing her hot forehead, trying to restrain her wild convulsions, when I looked up to see her sister standing in the doorway, peering at us.

'Go to bed,' I said as calmly as I could, trying to reassure the frightened child. 'She'll be better soon.'

'Is she going to die?'

I soothed Jennet, holding one of her burning hands in mine. 'Of course not, she'll be better in the morning, you'll see.'

'I took her to the village, it will be my fault.' Wild sobs burst from her, shaking her thin shoulders. 'I'm a wicked girl. I saw you and that man in the summer house and told Papa. I told him that you'd often met him there before.' I heard her clear young voice, but all my attention was with the sick child on the bed, and Elizabeth's words hardly reached me, seemed of no importance.

'It doesn't matter,' I told her and, at that moment, it was true. The future seemed far ahead and very uncertain.

Day and night merged and became one. Jennet tossed and turned, her once bonny cheeks were sunken, while her eyes grew hollow and shadowed with deep purple. With a determination I had not known I possessed, I fought for her life and at last the spots appeared but, even so, I dare not relax. Her fever scarcely abated and now the dreadful irritation came to plague her and I had to tie her hands to restrain her from disfiguring her face with her nails.

The days passed and I knew, with a sigh of relief, that she would live. I threw her linen in a bundle out of the window and it was dragged away to be burned but I knew she would not be free from infection until all the dried blisters had fallen from her skin. With relief from worry, I relaxed and allowed myself to grow weary. Elizabeth left her prison but, to be safe, I refused to allow anyone else to nurse Jennet, contenting myself with glimpses of Mally and Hal as they played in the garden below.

Jennet was a good patient, usually content to lie still or sleep while I sewed or read, but one day she was unusually fretful, keeping me busy until late in the evening, when she fell asleep and I was free to do all the jobs that had been left during the day. I tended the fire, kneeling on the floor and, leaning my aching head against the wooden surround, fell asleep with weariness, not waking when the door opened, only becoming aware of someone in the room when footsteps crossed the floor.

With a gasp of surprise, I jumped to my feet, caught my foot in the hem of my dress and would have fallen had not strong arms held me against a man's chest. For a moment I allowed myself to lie there, while my tired head swam, then recalling the circumstances, I pushed against the redcoat.

'No—no!' I cried, 'you should not be here!'

'Peace, be still. I took the smallpox as a child.'

A shuddering sigh escaped me, as I leaned against my husband, unwilling to stand on my own feet lest he took his comforting arms away and returned to his former stern self.

'I came as soon as I received Meg's letter.'

''Tis over now. An she regains her strength we have nothing to fear.'

Together we looked down at the sleeping child and I heard her father catch his breath at the sight of her frailness. His hand found mine and held it hard.

'I have much to thank you for,' he said quietly as we turned away.

During the weeks I had been incarcerated in the bedchamber, spring had come and I dared to open the window letting in the fresh sweet air of evening. We stood together in the casement, a slight breeze lifting the tendrils of hair from my neck and cooling my flushed cheek. After a while I sat on the windowseat and then Captain Everton took my chin in his hand and scrutinised my upturned face.

'And you, Anne, how fare you?'

'The better for seeing you,' I answered, glancing at him from under my lashes to see

197

how he took my words.

Grey eyes met and held mine as he searched my face. Deliberately I let him see something of what I felt and I saw his expression soften.

'Anne...' Seating himself beside me, he possessed himself of my hands. 'Elizabeth has confessed that the tales she told me were untrue.' Dropping my hands he took my shoulders and turned me towards him. 'All these weeks I wanted to apologise for what I said to you—for what I thought. Can you forgive a jealous man?'

I caught my breath. 'Jealous?' I asked softly, liking the thought, for to be jealous one must feel certain emotions, even though it be but possession.

'So jealous, Anne, that I wanted to kill him—and hurt you.'

'But you spared him. You had him at your feet—and spared him.'

His eyes dropped and he fell to toying with my fingers. I leaned forward. 'Because I asked it of you?' I queried softly.

'I couldn't kill a man you loved in front of you,' he said harshly.

'My dear, oh my dear.' I turned my hand and held his fingers, pulling them against my breast. 'I've never loved Ashley. I thought I did once, but I learned a while ago that it was infatuation, call it what you will, but never love.'

He was very still. 'Then why did you stay, if

198

it was not to save his life?' he asked slowly in tones of one who dares to hope.

'Must I say?' I asked, suddenly shy, half fearful of betraying what I had fought against and hidden for so long.

'I fear you must.'

Instead of answering him, I stared dreamily out into the dusky garden. 'All these years, since first you rode under the gatehouse, and I didn't know. For a long time I thought I hated you.'

'You had much to hate me for.'

'Not you, 'twas the war.'

'And yet without the war, we might never have met.'

I had to ask. 'And that would have been a bad thing?'

He looked at me. 'What think you Anne?' he countered quietly and waited inexorably for my reply.

Wordlessly, I lifted his brown hand and laid my cheek against it. At once I was in his arms, held tightly against his swiftly beating heart.

'I'll answer for you,' he whispered into my hair. ''Twould have been the most damnable thing, my love.'

And then I could say, 'I love you,' as I lifted my mouth for his kiss, finding security and much more besides in his arms. In these uncertain times no-one knows what the future might hold but, at least, we could face it together ... The Roundhead soldier and Cavalier lady that united held hope for the peace of our poor kingdom.

We hope you have enjoyed this Large Print book. Other Chivers Press or G.K. Hall & Co. Large Print books are available at your library or directly from the publishers.

For more information about current and forthcoming titles, please call or write, without obligation, to:

Chivers Press Limited
Windsor Bridge Road
Bath BA2 3AX
England
Tel. (01225) 335336

OR

G.K. Hall & Co.
P.O. Box 159
Thorndike, Maine 04986
USA
Tel. (800) 223–2336

All our Large Print titles are designed for easy reading, and all our books are made to last.